Praise for A Better World

"...The author successfully illustrates how the generational shift from traditional, old world values to materialism and immaturity has evolved..." —*The US Review of Books*

"Provocative, disturbing group of novellas that humanize international problems of violence and the plight of refugees."
—*Kirkus Reviews*

"She has an exquisite ear for dialogue that resonates in the present and whilst Saja, Yonna and Taraji each have their own unique stories, fate has set them on a common path, their thoughts proving timely revelations that will leave many readers reflecting deeply on our universal need for belonging, peace and happiness."

—*Book Viral*

"The author uses rich descriptions and authentic terminology to make each woman's world real for the reader. A Better World will appeal to readers who enjoy books that highlights the strengths of women or who like to root for the down-and-out."
—*IndieReader*

"A Better World is a great read for anyone looking for a story featuring women beating the odds."
—*Readers' Favorite*

A BETTER WORLD

a novel

BELANGELA G. TARAZONA

Also by Belangela G. Tarazona

The Child of Dawn
At the Confessional and Other Calamities
What No One Knew of the Dead Man
Presumed Indecent: The Story of Maruja Colina
Truths of Illusion, Volume 1
Noah Goes To School

All of the above are also available in Spanish.

in Danish
Daggryets Barn

Copyrights

Cover design: Norcki
Copyrights holder: Belangela G. Tarazona
Copyright © 2014 by Belangela G. Tarazona
ISBN 978-87-997379-4-9

Dedicated to my children in heaven and on earth

Acknowledgments

Preben, thanks for your loving support and for believing in this book, sometimes more than I myself did. I cannot be grateful enough for every Sunday you took care of Noah so I could finish this novel.

I would also like to send a word of appreciation to all the beta readers, for their valuable comments and suggestions.

My gratitude goes to the Scribendi team for polishing this manuscript before it could make its way to the readers.

Contents

Saja

Chapter 1

(2010)
Trincomalee - Sri Lanka

TO CALM DOWN, I stepped aside from the queue to observe those who were about to walk on the glowing coals, but this sudden agitation weighed in my stomach as if I had swallowed a whole coconut.

The smell of incense filled the air. The cries of those who had already crossed the plume of smoke, the rumble of the drums that the *melakaar*[1] beat in ecstatic rhythm, and the whistle of the flutes could not relax me, quite the contrary. We waited for our turn to walk on fire, the highest expression of spiritual purification.

I would have loved to skip this ritual, but my presence here was to test my faith, to speak to the oracle; I needed answers.

A woman was holding a child in her arms. She glanced up at the sky and mumbled something before taking the smoky trail. She ran almost on tiptoe as she clutched the girl to her chest. I thought that she smiled but actually, she gritted her teeth, probably to mask the pain. She gazed back as she reached the stairs, checked her feet, and smirked as she joined the huge throng on their way to the temple.

Standing behind the woman was a hunched man. His silver hair contrasted with his skin blackened by the sun; his fingers, deformed by arthritis, pressed the handle of a cane he used as a walking stick. The edge of his *sarong* licked the flames while he was passing; I thought for

---

1   A glossary of foreign terms is available

a second that the fire would devour the piece of cloth wrapping his torso. But despite his weary steps, he managed to reach the other side unscathed.

A tall, sturdy-looking man was next, his hair shiny, thanks to coconut oil. His *sarong* reached his calves. He stood before the bed of red-hot coals, which he briefly touched with a bunch of leaves he was holding, and he touched his forehead with it, emulating the movement of a handheld fan. He disappeared into the smoke to reappear seconds later at the foot of the stairs.

I did not have to roll up the hem of my *shalwar kameez* pants when my turn came, as they barely covered my ankles. I took the first step over the bed of hot cinders while the smoke made me cough.

Clouds like specks of lavender shades covered the sun; I noticed that not even the crows flew these skies. I hurried my footsteps to avoid burning my feet and exhaled in relief when it was over.

Once inside the temple, I peeked around, searching for Nalini and Shyamati, angels I no longer saw as friends, after many years they became my blood, my sisters and stood there, waiting for me next to a golden column.

"Did it hurt?" they asked as I approached them.

I shook my head. "It's like walking on the shells at noon, when the sun shines in the sky like an egg yolk on Nilaveli beach," I shouted, since the bustle of the drums outside drowned out our voices.

"Let's see the oracle," Shyamati suggested, handing me the bag I had given her when I joined the queue.

I pulled the pot with the flower from the bag, careful not to ruin the roots that discreetly climbed around the edges. We headed for the oracle.

We arrived in a crowded room where everyone was sitting on the floor. The air was heavy with the scents of jasmine and incense. We sat as quietly as we could and waited for our turn.

I WAS AWARE that maybe I could not speak to the oracle, since in June last year, shortly after Thani, my beloved husband, had disappeared in the white van, I had come with a pair of *chandbalis* of 22-carat gold encrusted with rubies and diamonds, which had been a wedding present from my *amma*, one of the last traces of my fancy life.

I was willing to give them the earrings as an offering, but the oracle had no time to talk to me back then. That alone told me that the oracle was not interested in money.

To think that once I had it all ... those memories now seemed futile.

THIS TIME, my offerings were five guavas, jasmine flowers, the silver tray we received on our wedding day, and the most cherished orchid I had been growing for the last three years, in loving memory of all that my *amma* represented in beauty and patience.

Thani had to come back because we had many outstanding plans, many outstanding kisses. The rest of our lives was now hanging, unfinished. Thani had to come back to fill our home with the joy that would only come from children. We had promised to bring a *pooja* to the frangipani tree on Swami Rock to foster fertility.

I had to see him again so I could give him all the gifts I had been hoarding as the ultimate proof that I had never forgotten our vows.

I was torn between reality and what my heart wanted me to believe. There was little indication that Thani was still alive, especially after I had read the letter that I received from the Criminal Investigation Department (CID).

In those times when no one would freely step into a police station alone, I came with a picture of my husband, inquiring as to his whereabouts. The CID sent me home empty-handed but made sure I received a letter days later, in which they denied any presence of detainees from the university. I still wished he had been arrested somewhere and that someday, he would come back. Someday, I would take his hands and tell him that I was willing to wait as long as he thought I should wait.

"Saja, I think the oracle wants to talk to you," Nalini whispered.

"Me?" I asked in disbelief.

"Yes, his servant is beckoning in your direction," Shyamati added.

I looked at the oracle, and one of the men standing beside him made a brief hand movement, indicating that I should come closer. I packed the orchid carefully into the bag and rose from the ground slowly. I passed through the mass of people sitting on the floor until I reached the center of the room. The man stretched out his hand so I could give him the bag. He peeked inside, reached in, and pulled out the plant by the leaves that spread like tabs on each side of the stems.

He smiled at my horror, as I witnessed the treatment he gave to one of my precious flowers.

"Careful," I whispered.

"You grew it yourself?"

"Yes, yes," I said, putting my hand under the pot.

"What's its name?" he challenged me while stroking the mottled red spots on the yellow petals.

"Spider orchid," I said. "They are for the oracle," I added, pointing toward the man sitting on the floor.

"My wife says that this plant requires a lot of patience. It seldom flowers," the man confessed.

"I give it a good shower every other day, letting the water run through, only wetting the base of the stem." Trying not to sound preachy, I added, "It is a flower of moisture and shade."

He eyed me a couple of seconds and smiled.

"You can talk to the oracle," he said, stepping aside to let me sit on the floor.

Chapter 2

I DID AS told and sat on the floor. The oracle spoke in Sanskrit, the language of my parents. The man rocked back and forth, staring at the ceiling. Suddenly, he made me drink coconut water from his own hand. I clasped my hands in prayer as I ignored the drops dripping from my jaw to my chest.

"What do you want to know?" he asked, lowering his head to make me whisper the question in his ear.

"It's Thani, my husband. He was arrested at the university," I said with a dry throat, despite the coconut water I just drank. I continued, "The rector said that the military assured him that once they finished with the questioning, they would bring them all back. Since then, none of them has been seen. I went to the military, seeking my husband, and they sent me to the Criminal Investigation Department, where I went with a picture of Thani. They sent me a sealed letter stating that there were no detainees from the university."

The oracle nodded and asked, "When's his birthdate?"

"April 30, 1978," I answered, lowering my head.

"You said you have a picture of him ..."

"Yes," I replied, producing the same picture I had shown at the CID.

I handed over the photo, which the oracle saw for a split second only. He averted his glance from the image as if dazzled by a spotlight. The servants moved steadily among the people present.

The oracle took a deep breath, closed his eyes, and shook his head. Suddenly, the only sound I heard was the clink of his bangles. He reopened his eyes and gave me a blank gaze. My eyes tried to meet his, which were fixed somewhere around my neck.

A cold breath filled my stomach, and my heart drummed.

The oracle made a sign to the servant beside him to bend down so he could say something to him. The servant did as requested, nodded a few times, eyed me briefly, and kept nodding. The oracle waved his hand for the servant to speak.

"Go to the pyres and do the rituals. Use oil, honey, sandalwood, and rich fabrics: orange and white. Cover it all with straw and burn it, until it turns to ashes. It is time for him to rest in peace," the servant announced.

I covered my face with my cupped hands and felt a black veil cover my vision, giving me the impression of seeing silver sparks.

I did not cry because I had no tears left. I had spilled them all when I heard that Thani was arrested. I cried when I went to the CID, when I lit incense in the temple, and when I wrapped every present I would give him the day we would meet again. I cried myself to sleep every night and every morning when I opened my eyes to confirm that our home was empty. I wept with regret because I had never cried for my *amma* and my *appa* as I cried for Thani.

In fact, the memory of Thani never left me. My husband appeared in my dreams, surrounded by kids who were our children.

"What happened?" I asked, unable to recognize the low moan of my own voice.

"There is no trace of your husband, no smell, no heartbeat. Not even ashes," the oracle told me, as he rocked impatiently. "Stop searching. He lies buried with others. Your husband didn't die alone," he concluded, biting his fist.

The assistant held out his hand to help me up but my legs refused to support me. I was broken with pain, clasped my hands in prayer, and let out a scream like the caw of a crow, which drew murmurs from those present. I bowed and finally managed to stand up.

The servant followed me to where Nalini and Shyamati sat. As I returned to my friends, the servant stared at my chin. I instinctively put my hand around my neck and felt the *thaali*. It had become part of my

6

skin; that's how I realized what the oracle was trying to tell me.

I should not be wearing the bridal necklace with emeralds and rubies that Thani had put around my neck the day we married. The *thaali* should be removed the day a wife becomes a widow.

Chapter

I REMEMBERED LIKE it was yesterday. After the first wave, the sea receded, attracting tourists and locals alike to witness the show of naked shells and fish bouncing on the sand, dazed by the sudden lack of water. As the group of onlookers grew, attracted by what the water covered minutes before, something in my head kept telling me to ignore the wonder and run up, inland, toward the temple.

Shortly after, the second wave charged with the feral power of a stampede, as if a river of melted *jaggery* poured over us, destroying homes, shattering dreams.

I grabbed hold of something; how could I tell? The flow of water and debris coming from the coast dragged me, and when I thought I was about to die from the mixture of saltwater and sand I was swallowing, I stayed trapped in the branches of a tree.

Without any warning, the tide of ruins that at first pushed me forward began to retreat. Now the sea claimed its own vomit, trying to drag me into its guts with the force of a giant magnet.

I didn't know how long I remained there and had no idea how I brought myself down the tree. I made my way, stepping on corpses, destruction, and what had been streets. I arrived at the temple. To my surprise and relief, Thani was there, as mute with dread as myself.

When he spotted me, Thani rushed to wrap me with the first piece of clothing he found. Only at that moment did I realize that I had walked naked from the waist down. The *choli* was still covering my chest, but the sea had gulped the *sari* I wore before the tragedy.

We hugged in silence and did not dare to feel self-pity. After all, we were alive and we were together.

AS I SAW it, the tsunami reduced me to the size of a cardamom seed. For Thani, however, surviving the tsunami gave him a dangerous sense of immortality and the conviction that he could defeat any impossibility.

I had the impression that this idea strengthened as we heard the increasing death toll. It was the same feeling that had helped him digest the news that his parents were among the thousands of victims who perished, trapped in the carriages of a train on its way from Galle to Colombo.

THIS TIME, I did not have relatives to mourn, for my *amma* and my *appa* had passed away in 2007, in the hands of a mob who set fire to the hotel they owned, which had been in the family since my grandparents' youth. The enraged horde trampled the orchids and chanted. They looted what they could and shot dead anyone who did not speak Sinhala, the native language of the Sinhalese people.

In an attempt to avenge our parents, my *tamby* vowed family separation and joined the Liberation Tigers of Tamil. That was how he became a *poorali*, a warrior. Years later, I saw the picture of my younger brother on TV, cursed by the government and praised by the Tamils as a Black Tiger, whose blood nourished the mountains of Jaffna in a suicide attack.

Something told me now that both the authorities and my husband's recklessness killed him, as he never stopped talking in Tamil while in the presence of the Sinhalese people.

Although we had heard rumors of what was happening in the universities, he insisted that we Tamils would perish if we kept denying our culture.

IN THOSE DAYS, I hated my husband for his moral code and courage. Thani was the last root tying me to Sri Lanka; otherwise, I would have stayed in Europe, making good use of my hard-earned credentials.

If he had been more cowardly, I would not be heading to India as a refugee, on board an illegal fishing boat. My only assets were the *chandbalis,* which I had not been able to offer to the oracle, and the *thaali.* I thought about taking a handful of sand with me as a piece of this side of the world but changed my mind when I heard the boat's engine coughing like a tubercular on his deathbed.

"May you and your family have a long life," I wished Shyamati in a voice filled with sadness. She was the faithful friend who had offered me her wholehearted affection despite knowing that I was Tamil.

"Hurry up, Saja. They're comin'," she said, looking over her shoulder toward the village.

We heard the shooting wounding the sky, and torches shone like sparks in the distance. I saw into her eyes and hugged her. Someone from one of the boats prompted me to hurry up and I came on board knowing that we probably would not survive the journey to the other side. But what else could we do?

That night, two boats sailed northward.

Chapter 4

Refugee camp — Denmark

"SAJA, BELIEVE ME when I tell you that we want to help you but every time we talk, the story is different," remarked Vinnie Holm, flipping through the pages in her notepad.

"The first time, you said you came to Europe on a fishing boat that fell apart like wet paper only hundreds of yards offshore," she read, paused, and met my eyes.

As I did not utter any comment, she continued reciting my stories.

"The second time, you said you came to Europe from Canada but when we contacted the immigration service in Ottawa, there was no Saja who had arrived by air or who matched your description."

"I don't even remember how I ended up here," I said, my eyes glued to the floor.

"I'll refresh your memory 'cos that's all we can confirm from the police," said Vinnie. Her red curls shook as she made the slightest nod.

"The police picked you up at the train station in Copenhagen. The only thing you kept saying was *refugee*. That's why you're here."

I remained silent so as not to worsen matters but my memories were like putting chopped onions and diced carrots in a broth of *mulligatawny*, where the riots in Colombo in which my parents died, the tsunami, Thani's disappearance, and the quest to reach Denmark swam in the same pot.

"Saja?"

"Yes?"

"Do you have something to say?" she pressed.

I shook my head. I wanted to gather my thoughts. I examined the room and noticed the white, trumpet-shaped lamp hanging from the ceiling, the light wood veneer of gray Formica on top of the table, and the matching chairs covered with a kind of blue cloth made of something similar to wool that made my legs itch.

On the far wall hung a bulletin board overlaid with yellow Post-its, and next to it, a corkboard for hanging keys. To the right was a window along the wall, displaying rows of barracks housing hundreds of families in the same situation as mine.

I did not remember whether the fatigue had hit me shortly after the funeral rites or when I embarked on my journey to flee from Sri Lanka. The truth was that the pain in my stomach had become perennial. I thought it was due to hunger but whenever my hunger was satiated, the pain kept returning so I could not sleep, until I heard someone saying that fatigue can also produce a stomach ache.

I was exhausted but nights passed when I was unable to even close my eyes.

Thani's image became so real that I saw him arriving home, with kids running around him. When I reached out to welcome them, they broke into tiny pieces of porcelain that scattered around the floor and turned into *vibhuti*, sacred ashes.

I covered my face with my hands and tried to cry; I really wanted to cry, but I had forgotten how.

"Saja?" The woman asked in an attempt to make me stay in the present.

I lifted my head as I winced in pain.

"Saja, okay, let's talk about something else," she said, straightening up on the chair. "Tell us about your family."

"I'm tired," I said, clutching my belly.

"Are you tired or hungry?" she asked when she saw my hands clutching my stomach.

"I'm tired," I replied without raising my head.

14

She was about to protest but the uniformed man sitting next to her whispered something in her ear. She nodded resignedly and announced, "Okay, let's leave it for today. We will contact the doctor and ask him to examine you soon. But you have to go to the infirmary, as the medical staff don't usually go to the barracks. Are you strong enough to sit in the waiting room?"

I nodded. The truth was that I would have said yes to anything, just to be left alone and to jump into bed. I wanted to be alone but it was a mixed feeling because when I was on my own, the images of my past assailed me and I wanted to have someone close, someone who would not question me. Someone who would just hold me and promise that I was no longer in danger.

"It would be good for you to write about your family and what you recall," Vinnie advised, ripping off the pages of notes she had written on the pad and handing me the rest with the pen on top. "We can talk when you feel better," she said, standing up. The police officer sitting next to her followed her.

When they left, I stood from the chair to drink water from the cooler at the back of the room, but a woman wearing a red vest with the Red Cross logo offered to drive me to the barracks in a green cart like those used in a golf course.

To hell with the infirmary; I'll do that tomorrow.

ONCE IN MY room, I closed the door and jumped into bed, still holding the notebook and the pen. I wanted to remember as much as I could to end the agony of these interviews. I closed my eyes for a second but images of torches, the rite in the pyres, and people gulped by the sea materialized as if I were watching a movie. I felt like a voodoo doll; every memory was a pin that fate viciously stuck into me.

I opened my eyes and stared at the ceiling. Like a flash, it occurred to me that the police were only interested in knowing the route I had taken to reach Europe. Anyway, I could not remember precisely, but I realized that if I gave them the details, maybe they would do everything possible to prevent someone else from escaping whatever hell they were running away from, and I could not help them do that.

I prayed for the wind to take my memories away so I did not have to lie when I said I did not remember how I ended up at the Central Station.

I sat on the edge of the bed and wrote about my grandparents, who were from Chennai. I also made notes about my parents and what happened to them in Colombo. I described my studies at Red River College in Manitoba and the training course on *nouvelle cuisine* that I had taken in Lyon.

I related that my parents had wanted me to get married, but as time passed and I could not find a suitable candidate, I left them to take charge. I recounted how we had discarded the first suitor, as he was not vegetarian like me. I also explained that the second man rejected me for fear that I was "too modern," due to my studies in Canada and France. The third candidate turned me down on the grounds of incompatible horoscopes. Finally, Thani came along.

I liked him and he also liked me. He could not have cared less about horoscopes and saw my years abroad as an asset. My *amma* and my *appa* jumped with delight, since Thani, like us, was *Iyengar Brahmin*.

More than once, I told my parents jokingly that they did not arrange our marriage. The stars did.

Chapter

5

Refugee camp—Denmark

I IMMERSED MYSELF in writing what I could remember of my own story and gleefully noticed that my stomach ache became milder.

I jumped out of bed and sat by the coffee table, facing the wall to keep writing. I had to turn on the lamp as the lights from outside suddenly dimmed. I had a roommate who did not talk much, though I had not seen her in recent days. On her bed was a piece of paper with the Red Cross logo, which said, "COME TO OFFICE" in capital letters. I observed the landscape out of the window; red clouds covered the sky behind the row of barracks across the street.

It was pure luck that I had ended up in the family section of the camp, as the single women's area was so crowded that the staff had no other choice but to place some of us here. I'd heard that there was very little room for four people and that one had to share the always-busy toilets along the corridors. The Red Cross had placed trailer toilets outside to alleviate the situation. I had had no chance to corroborate it myself, but if what I'd heard at the cafeteria was true, the stench was so overpowering that it equaled the putrid odors passersby would smell when strolling through the alleys of Dharavi.

I went to the bathroom and filled a glass with tap water. I looked up at the mirror and it hit me how haggard I appeared. I was a sad, emaciated woman, with parchment-like skin and matted hair. The dark circles under my eyes reminded me of the raccoons I had seen in Manitoba. My skin hung loosely on my cheeks, giving me a ghostly appearance, which made me think of the lines from a poem by R. Tagore that I had read years ago:

My life when young was like a flower
—a flower that loosens a petal or two from her abundance and never feels the loss when the
spring breeze comes to beg at her door.

I tried to remember the rest but the words must have disappeared in the fog of my tragedies. I certainly had lost not just a petal or two but hundreds. As far as I was concerned, there was no hint of a spring breeze begging at my door.

I put my open palm on the mirror to cover the aged woman's image reflected there.

I drank the water in the glass in one gulp and returned to the table to write.

I could not help pouring out onto those pages the nature of my marriage, which was a beautiful garden full of plants: bougainvilleas, kamalas, begonias, *ambal,* roses, and *tamarai.* I whispered my wishes to the buds, took great care to remove dead leaves, fertilized the soil from time to time, and watered the plants at the end of the day, when the sun no longer burned the earth.

I was filled with joy to watch my husband writing, preparing his lessons. I loved the expression on his face when I served my culinary experiments with *avarakkai kootu, vazhaipoo usili, brinjals,* and *upma kozha kattai.* It was wonderful when we walked hand in hand on the shore of Nilaveli beach or when we invited Nalini and Shyamati over to enjoy dinner.

Years passed and we were not blessed with children. The flowers, apparently in solidarity with my infertility, also refused to bloom, not even the grateful bougainvillea, which required so little care. Orchids came into my garden when my *amma* died. It was a tribute to her and her patience, and I swore to make them bloom, even if it only happened once.

Fortunately, I did not have to wait that long before the flowers opened. I thought it was the signal bringing the blessing of children.

THE PAIN IN my stomach returned. It seemed as if my guts squirmed deep inside me, making me bend in pain. I realized that it was too late to go to the cafeteria to have something to eat, so I took a deep breath and closed my eyes. When the tide of pain was over, I resumed my writing.

It was after midnight when I finished. I folded the wad of sheets to hand them over first thing in the morning. Anyway, I had to see the doctor as Vinnie had suggested. I did not expect that this written material could help my case; I only knew that I was Saja, a woman who had loved a man named Thani, whose demise had smashed any hope of starting a family.

(2011)
Immigration Service, Copenhagen

IN THE CONFERENCE room at the Danish Immigration Service, those invited to a follow-up meeting had spent hours discussing pending cases. Walls painted in stark white dazzled, in contrast to the gray skies threatening with rain. Two joined tables stood in the center of the room, providing seating for fifteen people. Two lamps with aluminum screens hung together from the ceiling, in between an overhead projector that reflected images on a viewing screen in front of the audience.

On the table were Thermos containers of coffee and tea. Sorted by colors, the teabags rested in a red wooden box saying LIPTON in golden letters.

"These are the last three cases left we still need to discuss," Vinnie said, operating the remote pointer. The picture of a woman with heavy makeup was displayed on screen.

"She's a Colombian national but flew via Amsterdam. She says her name is Eugenia Restrepo but the passport is fake, and we suspect that she is running away from some prostitution ring in the red district."

"Have you guys contacted someone in Holland?" asked Mads Lambeck, a tall, massive man, one of those who invested many hours of his leisure time lifting weights at the gym. He was the man, the boss of bosses. He reported directly to the minister so he was entitled to demand information.

"We made contact but haven't heard much."

"Any idea of how long it will take them?" he asked, taking notes.

"Tough to say; my best guess would be about a month."

Mads nodded and Vinnie clicked the button of the pointer. "Keep track of this, please."

She clicked on the pointer again, showing the picture of a man wearing a black cowboy hat, with pitch-black, elongated eyes and a nose that was a reduced version of an eagle's beak. The shape of his mouth was impossible to see, as a smooth moustache covered the whole area down to his lower lip, spreading over his beard.

"His name is Punka Sahili and he says he's from Uzbekistan, no papers. The police found him up in Elsinor, near the train station."

"If he didn't carry any ID, how come you guys know he's from Uzbekistan?"

"We don't believe that story, and even though he requested asylum, we're almost sure he isn't interested in the residence permit."

"How so?"

"We think he's Romani. Our theory is that he's a pickpocket and is here for the free stay. When his application gets rejected, he moves on to someplace else."

"And all this is based on what?"

"It's just a hunch," she admitted.

"We don't work based on hunches; we need to establish his identity," Mads warned her. "What do you have in mind to find out?"

"Horse meat," she replied matter-of-factly.

"Pardon?" he asked; all raised their heads and paid attention.

"Yes, to Romani people, horses are considered almost holy, and it would be a serious offense to eat horse meat. We are going to invite him for a meal and make him believe that what he's eating is juicy, tender horse beef. We hope his reaction will give him away," she said with a mischievous smile.

"Brilliant," Mads said; the compliment made her blush.

"Thanks," she said, clicking on the pointer for the third time, displaying the picture of a woman with dark circles under her eyes and with black hair parted in the middle and pulled back in a tight chignon.

"She is Saja. She claims that her family was killed in Colombo and her husband was taken in a raid at the university where he taught. She is running away from the recent outbreaks of violence."

"ID?"

"Nothing. We forwarded her fingerprints and a picture of her to the UNHCR in Mandapam with the hope that they can give any clues on her. We're almost sure she came from Tamil Nadu."

"How many times have you guys interviewed her?"

"Two times; on both occasions, she told different stories. We had to suspend the last interview because Saja complained of stomach pains. The doctor saw her and said that those might be symptoms of post-traumatic stress. He prescribed antidepressants to help her sleep. Everything seems to hold, except for her age. How old do you think she says she is?" Vinnie asked everyone in the room.

"Forty," the boss ventured.

"What about you guys?" She encouraged the rest of the audience.

"Between forty and forty-two," said another colleague.

"Okay, how old is she?" the boss pressed.

"She says she's twenty-nine." Vinnie smiled at the crescendo of comments after her revelation.

"Yes, and she also claims to be a graduate from Red River College in Manitoba and to have taken a course in an institute of *nouvelle cuisine* in France."

"So you believe her?" Mads asked, jotting down on the notebook.

"It could be, judging by her perfect English. The only problem is the age issue. That's what we want to challenge; we are even considering having a doctor check her to determine her age."

"Have you contacted Red River College?"

"And the Paul Bocuse Institute," said Vinnie, finishing the sentence for him. "We are waiting for their response."

"If I may interrupt ...," said Peter Frederiksen, who until now had not wanted to give an input, given Mads' bossy attitude.

The boss took advantage of the interruption to refill his cup.

"Go ahead, Peter," Vinnie encouraged him.

"Did you say the Paul Bocuse Institute?"

"Well ... I don't know if I pronounced it well; I don't speak French," she said apologetically, "but if you want to read her notes," she offered as she approached with the sheets she had received from Saja.

Peter flipped through them and smiled. "I could help," he said.

"How?"

"I know the Paul Bocuse Institute."

"Really? And what does a project manager from the asylum office know about Paul Bocuse?" Vinnie asked, smiling. Now everyone's eyes were on Peter.

"You know Erica, my ex. She did a course there and I visited her a couple of times," he explained, blushing.

Chapter

7

(2011)

EVERY TIME I heard the word "office" from the Red Cross staff, I panicked, since it could be that they had rejected my application or would send me to another facility or much worse, that the authorities would send me back to Sri Lanka.

Without much explanation, they handed me an envelope with the Immigration Service letterhead and continued their rounds of the other barracks.

Rarely did the staff deliver letters; these rounds were usually to check whether people were still using the rooms. So when they gave me the letter, I opened it with shaky hands.

I dropped it on the floor. I took a deep breath, picked it up, and opened it slowly. To my dismay, the letter was written in Danish.

I read the name carefully to make sure the letter was addressed to me. I did not know if I should blow my nose with it or simply make a Napoleon hat.

"How on earth can I understand what is written on this paper, since I do not speak Danish?" I mumbled furiously.

I put my shawl on and went to see if someone at the main entrance could help me decipher the meaning of the letter.

I walked through the barracks and noticed that the grass needed a sweet, loving hand. It grew as uneven as the fur of a stray dog. I passed by a boy who was sitting on a green milk crate as he fiddled with a cell

25

phone.

At the main entrance, a tired-looking man took the letter, checked both sides as if assessing how many pages he had to translate, and proceeded to explain. In the distance, a police siren could be heard. The man shrugged as he turned his head in the direction of the noise.

"There's nothin' to worry about," he smiled. "You're invited to a meeting at the Immigration Service. It also says who will be present." He handed me back the letter.

He wrote down the date and time; I thanked him and walked away. I thought about going directly to the barracks as I realized that it was nearly noon, so I decided to go to the cafeteria and avoid the long lines, which usually took away my hunger.

It was also a bad idea to walk alone in the camp, as one might become prey to other refugees. I guess I was lucky; I had the appearance of a wreck so no one wished to mess with me, but I had heard rumors of what was going on in the corridors of the single women's area. Since then, I had carried with me the grill knife that I had received, along with other items, the day I first came to the camp.

The yellow building with white windows housed the cafeteria. When you approached, the sign of a fork and knife next to the main door welcomed you to a long box, where you had to stand in line to the right. I thought that I was one of the first to arrive but about thirty people were already holding their trays.

The camp sheltered a wide range of nationalities, and the air carried the sounds of unpronounceable languages, like a little Babel in Scandinavia. In front of me were two young women who spoke broken English. Judging by their appearance, I would say they were from Eastern Europe. I was certain that they were not from the same country. Otherwise, they would be speaking in their native tongue.

They were chatting about the police sirens I had heard at the main entrance. The police had come to stop someone who had run amok after learning that the Immigration Service had rejected his application. In a fit of despair, he had begun to toss possessions through his window. Apart from the broken glass, no one was injured.

I sent him a friendly thought since it could be me next time. But what else could we do? There was no use worrying about others' fates when I did not have a surplus of mental resources to handle my own situation.

I noticed that people talked animatedly as they stood in line. But once the food was served, one searched for a place to sit and devoured everything as soon as possible, as if it were a competition, without noticing who was sitting by one's side, without uttering the slightest comment. We were like automatons; we stood in line, someone from the kitchen served the rations on the trays, and we ate and left, only to repeat the same ritual at the next meal.

The show was daunting but I depended on the cafeteria because only refugees with children obtained a certain amount of cash to buy their own food.

Chapter

AS I ENTERED the meeting room, I recognized Vinnie Holm. With her were a stern-faced woman and a young man from the Immigration Service. The fourth person was a blond lady, whose role in the interview I did not quite understand.

Vinnie offered a translator, whom I politely refused, since the conversation could well be conducted in English.

After the introductions, I learned that the man's name was Peter Frederiksen, the short, dark-haired woman with the severe expression called herself Lone Wagner, and the blond woman only said her first name: Erica.

Vinnie took the floor.

"Saja, thank you very much for the notes you wrote," she said, as she produced a sheaf of papers from her briefcase.

I nodded, waiting for the interrogation. My left foot furiously pumped an imaginary pedal to ease the anxiety building up in my stomach. I took a bottle of water available on the table.

"This is the last interview, Saja. The notes we take today, plus what the police have gathered, will form the basis for the decision on your asylum application. It normally takes about three months but that could be extended, depending on how long it takes to receive the information from the authorities in other countries, okay?" she explained, like I was a little girl.

"Yes," I said, removing the plastic cap from the bottle.

"You said you attended Red River College in Manitoba, didn't you?"

"Yes."

"What did you study, Saja?"

"Culinary arts," I answered, wiping my mouth with the back of my hand after my sip of water.

"Was it under the creative arts program?" Vinnie asked as she glanced at Erica.

"No," I said, frowning. "As far as I know, the only way to study culinary arts at Red River is through the hospitality program."

Vinnie exchanged glances with Erica, who nodded. Vinnie wrote notes as she asked me, "Do you remember in what year that was?"

"Yes, it was 1999."

"You remember how old you were in 1999?"

"I must have been about 17," I replied, without taking my eyes from the bottle of water I was holding.

"How long were you in Manitoba?"

"Almost two years."

"That was until which year ..." She stopped in mid-sentence to let me fill in the gap.

"2001."

"What did you do afterwards?"

"What everyone else in that program was doing. I submitted an application to the Paul Bocuse Institute. You see, the institutions have an exchange agreement. If you make it to the course, you join the high ranks of the *nouvelle cuisine*. The diploma of completion opens many doors."

"So you were accepted?"

"Yes, and I finished."

"What do you mean?"

"Not all who enter finish the course."

After this comment, I noticed that Erica shot a nasty glance at me as she crossed her arms. Was it rage? Why? Peter, who was sitting to her right, gave her a gentle pat on the arm. Her reaction worried me a little bit, as I didn't know her role in all this. I wondered what I could have said that made her so furious.

"How long did it take?" Vinnie asked. "Saja, are you with us?" she prodded when I did not respond.

"Sorry, I didn't hear."

"How long did it take?"

"Oh, yes, four months."

"What did you do next?"

"I went back to Colombo."

"Do you remember what year that was?" Vinnie asked as she grabbed a bottle of water from the table.

"Yes, in 2002."

"Saja, how old were you in 2002?"

"Twenty," I said, meeting her eyes, annoyed at her suspicion.

"Could you tell us what happened when you arrived in Colombo?" she asked, softening her tone.

I took another sip of water because my tongue stuck to my gums, as if smeared with glue.

"The agreement with my *parents* was that they would let me finish my education and if I wasn't engaged upon my return to Colombo, they would try to find a suitor for me."

"What did you do?"

"I let them take over; anyway, I would have the last word."

"Sorry, in what year did you go back to Colombo?"

"As I said before, at the beginning of 2002."

I noticed that Vinnie was cross-questioning me to test if I was lying. I took another sip of water.

"You claim you are a widow; do you remember in which year you got married?"

"2003, in May."

"How old were you in 2003?"

"Twenty-one."

"Saja, when were you born?"

"I was born on April 14, 1982."

"Meaning that today you would be ..." She raised her head, waiting for my answer.

"*Today* I'm twenty-nine," I finished the sentence, stressing "today."

"Aha," she said and observed me while scratching her head with the pen. She added, "Saja, let's face it; you're not what I could call a twenty-nine-year-old woman," as she rested the pen on the notebook.

"That explains why I avoid mirrors," I answered without thinking. The anxiety was long gone, replaced by a fit of rage I was having a hard time controlling.

A heavy silence fell over the room; I realized that her gaze wasn't of compassion but of triumph. She thought that she had caught me at fault, that I was lying.

Having nothing left to lose, I fired back, "Do you think I come from a beach resort? In 2007, a crazed mob killed my parents in Colombo; consequently, my brother joined the Tigers of Tamil and took the vow of family separation. This *freshness* of my complexion," I said, drawing circles around my face, "is due to the tsunami of 2004, where we lost everything. For those who were *Iyengar Brahmin*, meaning upper cast in Sri Lanka it would not have been appropriate to accept the government's help to rebuild our homes."

As no one opened their mouths to interrupt, I continued listing the misfortunes that had contributed to my withered appearance.

"Another thing that helps with wrinkles is to know that the government is killing civilians in its race to finish off the Tigers. Worms ate Thani's body because he was buried in a mass grave somewhere between Trincomalee and Batticaloa. On top of it, I ran away like a fugitive on an illegal fishing boat, which shattered hundreds of meters off the coast of Rameshwaram.

"We were lucky to make it to the shore, but the other boat fell apart somewhere near Point Pedro. Right there! Before our eyes! And we couldn't help them, since just one extra passenger would have meant sinking our own boat. We saw them disappear in the water, one by one. The horror painted on each of their faces will stay forever imprinted on my mind," I said, lowering my head, as I could feel the moisture in my eyes. But no tears would run down.

"Saja, excuse me, I didn't mean to upset you," said Vinnie, as she covered her mouth with her fist to stifle a sneeze.

"I know; you're just doing your job."

The pause became so uncomfortable that I took another sip from the bottle. I scanned the room and spotted Erica toying with a golden lock of her hair that hung from one side of her temple. When we made eye contact, her gaze hardened and she rolled her eyes. Lone Wagner watched mesmerized, a pen in her hand. Peter was peeking at me on the sly; every time our eyes met, he lowered his head.

"Saja, can you tell us how you came to Europe?" Vinnie asked.

Her request came out in a low tone, like a mild attempt to resume the questions.

"What I remember is that," I took a deep breath, "Shyamati, my best friend, bought my place on the fishing boat. We sailed north from Trincomalee toward Mandapam, where there is a temporary refugee camp. I stayed there a few months but when we learned that they might bring us back to Sri Lanka, I decided to pay an agent to help me out of India. I would have preferred Canada or France but he suggested Denmark, since the passport control is far less rigorous than in those two countries."

"So you were carrying money with you?" Peter inquired.

"No, I only had two things of value: the *thaali* and the earrings, a present from my mother."

"*Thaali?*" he asked.

"Yes, a gold necklace with rubies and emeralds. I gave it to the agent to cover the flight ticket and the false passport. The agent made the trip with me. We split at the train station in Copenhagen, where he made me return my passport and the flight ticket. He instructed me to say 'refugee' when the police asked. The agent was right all along; no one stopped us at the airport."

"Do you remember the name of the agent?"

I smiled and shook my head. "He said his name was Arumuka Navalar."

"What is so funny?" Vinnie wanted to know.

"The name was fake. Of course, I didn't believe him, as Arumuka Navalar was a prominent Tamil who died in 1800. Actually, it was a relief that he lied about it. As far as I was concerned, I didn't want to know much about the nature of his business."

"It didn't worry you to hand over the only treasures you had?"

"What would you have done in my situation?"

Chapter

9

WHEN I CAME out of the interview, I was convinced that the Immigration Service would reject my application. At least I had bought some time before the final rejection. It was like someone had thrown ten years more over my shoulders. Not even the rumble in my stomach was incentive enough to have something to eat.

Time seemed to drag; every single second became a century. The days passed in the same routine: take three meals and wait. Wait and sit in the stands area of the stadium, not to watch a cricket match, but to watch my own life and the lives of those who would suffer the same fate as mine.

My life in the camp was reduced to keeping track of the quarrels between rival clans, watching the state of the man who had started a hunger strike as his case was rejected, watching the arrival of new refugees, and saying goodbye to those leaving, as they were allowed to stay or were relocated. Another hot conversation topic was deportees, who simply went underground.

To me, the refugee camp was a repository of broken souls. The fact of not knowing anything about my situation and being immersed in a system that was designed to keep me in absolute darkness was abhorrent. Worse yet was the fact that I did not have the opportunity to fill the hours with an activity, which could have given me a sense of direction.

Apart from the sewing room, the info café, a group of women, a bicycle shop, and the compulsory attendance in the orientation course, there was nothing I could use to learn a trade that would have allowed me to recover some of my lost dignity by being of service.

The feeling of having no control over my own destiny and the overwhelming sense of receiving alms were annihilating.

I decided to attend an English course, even though everyone said it was horrendous. Not because I needed it, but as a means of breaking the routine.

The course was an unfortunate parody, which many like me attended to kill time. The lack of motivation rose like a mist after rain, and the instructor ended up losing heart, too. We sat there, exchanging glances, browsing books, aiming at nothing. I did not know how it went for the rest, as I dropped it after the third class.

When I got off the bus after the course, I thought that maybe I could give a helping hand somewhere in the camp.

I did not want to think; I did not want to remember. The 25-mg Zoloft the doctor prescribed had helped, but I was convinced that the best antidepressant was to keep my mind busy.

"HELLO?" I CALLED, entering through the rear door of the cafeteria. A young man was coming from the opposite direction, holding two black trash bags. He signaled that I could talk to someone in the office.

I entered the narrow hallway and spotted the long dining tables at the other end. A blue-eyed petite woman met me.

She greeted me in Danish.

"Do you speak English?" I asked.

"Yes, yes."

"I wonder if you need someone to give a hand ..."

"No vacancies," she said, as she turned to go back to the office.

"I'm offering help for free."

"Sure?" she asked, stopping short.

"Not a nickel," I replied, smiling.

"Helping hand with anything?"

"Well ... anything related to the cafeteria."

"Sometimes we need help with the cafeteria trays; what do you say?"

"When do I start?"

Her eyes lit up. "As soon as possible. Oh, by the way, my name is Jeanette," she said as she reached out to shake my hand.

Chapter
10

EIGHT MONTHS HAD passed since the last interview, and I had not heard from the Immigration Service. Torn between doubts about whether or not it would be wise to call them for a follow-up, I told myself that sometimes, no news was good news. We had experienced that most of the cases that were resolved within a three-month timeframe were deportations.

I got out of bed with the first light and after a quick shower, off I went to help in the kitchen. I spent the days washing trays, cleaning tables after each meal, and taking out the trash. We usually started the day receiving the ingredients from the trucks; we had to check that the amounts were correct. If everything was fine, we stocked the items in the larder. I was also responsible for putting clean trays in place and checking that there were enough napkins.

So that was how I had been defeating the ghosts of the past, to the point that sometimes a whole week would go by without my taking a single Zoloft. I had no more dry mouth, either.

Jeanette had been giving me some more responsibilities. On the days when Mia, the pastry chef, did not show up, I took care of the baked goods. I was also tasked with peeling the potatoes and making the salads.

Mia had long hair, which she tied in two braids that she rolled on each side, in the way of the Bavarian waitresses at Oktoberfest. She hated the idea of my taking over her duties when she was absent and she voiced her displeasure whenever she could. Perhaps she was afraid that I would grab her job, which was completely ridiculous. I didn't even have a work permit.

When we were alone in the kitchen, Mia called me names in Danish. She slammed doors and threw pots and pans.

I sensed that she clenched her fists and tensed her body when I was around. Her displeasure toward me amused me. I wondered whether this was all because she saw me as a threat or whether this had a racist character.

I didn't really know what brought on so much anger in her, but her smile disappeared at the sight of me. I also spotted the wrinkles on her chin as if she was eating tamarind paste. I sensed, too, the quickened rhythm of the knife falling on the vegetables she was chopping.

If I stood close to her on my way to grab something near where she was standing, she stepped aside, taking care not to touch an inch of me, as if the color of my skin was going to leave a stain of soot on her white shirt. She mumbled something while rolling her eyes.

So far I had ignored her, because my goal was not to think. But I also took care to stay out of her way. I just wanted to be of use until my application was processed.

JEANETTE ANNOUNCED THAT the next day, she would run some personal errands and Mia would be in charge.

When I came the next day, I noticed that the rear door was wide open. I came in, hung up my jacket, and switched shoes to the black clogs Jeanette gave me when I started at the cafeteria. I took my apron and headed for the kitchen. An inviting scent of fresh coffee was wafting in the air.

"Hey, Black. Take a day off; we don't need you here," Mia barked.

"Black?" I repeated.

She did not answer. Instead she stepped forward and stood a few inches away from me, puffing out her chest like a pigeon; the only difference was that she was not courting. She stood there with arms akimbo, challenging me.

"What, you didn't hear me?" she said, and tiny drops of her saliva landed on my chest.

It was obvious that Mia knew nothing about Martin Luther King and his dream and that there was no way in hell we two could work in peace.

Now that I had my answer to why she hated me so much, I realized that I didn't give a hair of a dead mosquito whether she liked me or not. I grabbed a frying pan from a pile of utensils standing on the corner and banged it against the tabletop, but it crashed on the floor as it slipped from my hand.

Mia ran away and locked herself inside Jeanette's office, and I realized that I was done in this kitchen. I changed my clothes and left the cafeteria. I needed air.

ON MY WAY to the barracks, I toyed with the idea of what this path would look like with some cherry trees lining each side. Instead of the horrid fence with the barbed wire on top, what if the camp was surrounded by hundreds of bougainvilleas? I closed my eyes for a second, and the picture in front of me was heavenly. I could also hear the gentle sound of the wind sweeping and swirling the fallen flowers on both sides of the road.

I opened my eyes and reality hit me. There was no noise of flowers but the steps of a man, whom everyone called the gypsy; I recognized him by his hat. He kept an eye on me every time I was about to empty the tray trolley in the cafeteria. He managed to be right there by the trolley, and when I grabbed the trays from one end, he pulled them toward himself from the other end.

Rumor had it that he was a gypsy who wasn't even interested in getting asylum. People said that he was not staying long and that he just wanted to have a place to crash and eat for free. He would disappear when his case was rejected or if he got into trouble with the police, whichever happened first.

No one liked him, for he was taking the place of someone else who really needed asylum.

When he smiled, he seemed an orc worthy of *The Silmarillion*. I would stare back at him, as if my face was made of stone, and would wait until he released the trays. When he was done with his hideous game, I would

41

take the trays and walk away as soon as I could.

I suspect he had been watching me since I arrived at the camp. I had managed to shake him off so far, but I also had to admit that he was becoming more and more cheeky.

If I walk back, he will notice that I'm afraid of him.

I took a deep breath and tried to keep my pace. About ten feet away, I could hear him walking more slowly but still approaching. My eyes met his in a stern expression to discourage him.

"How come you are here so early?" I heard him say.

I did not answer. I smiled through clenched lips and kept going.

I searched around, hoping to catch a familiar face, but no one appeared. I spotted the fence in the background, where deer sometimes came to eat from the hands of some of us.

A mixture of ammonia smell and nicotine hit my nose.

"No time for a little chit chat?" he offered in broken English.

"Tired." It was all I replied, as I ran my hand down my waist to make sure that the grill knife that I always carried with me was in place.

Chapter

11

I ARRIVED AT my barracks with the feeling that the gypsy was right behind me. With shaky hands, I inserted my key into the keyhole but it fell to the ground on my first try. I glimpsed over my shoulder; there was no one. I took a deep breath and picked up the key. I opened the door and locked myself inside.

After analyzing the situation, I decided that it was wiser to stop helping in the cafeteria. I felt proud for not demeaning myself by hitting Mia with the frying pan, as her offenses paled in comparison with the threats I felt from the gypsy.

I would drop by to say goodbye to Jeanette and seek something else to do.

The women's club had been discarded because it was a nest of harpies. Besides, they had ruled me out on the grounds that I was a widow. They had even asked me how I made it to the camp without being raped.

I pulled back the curtain and opened the window; a damp smell of wet earth drifted in. It was from a sudden rain, which laid a thin layer of sadness on the deserted path. From here, the huge sandbox was visible, like a statement that it was there for the kids to play in. But they never used it or maybe I was not aware enough to see anyone playing there.

That sandbox could make a lovely pond with lotus flowers and a handful of goldfish, I imagined.

I sat on the edge of the bed, thinking about what I could do to fill the hours, and I just kept wondering what was going on with my application. I felt a rush of cold air in my stomach and sensed how the muscles at the base of my neck tightened.

I rubbed my shoulders and decided to take a shower, hoping to relax, but anxiety had taken over me once again. I opened my locker and took out the packet of Zoloft. I hated the pills because they gave me the sensation of eating sand, but I didn't want to lose hope, either. That was the only thing that kept me going, so I took the pastel green pill and swallowed it without water.

"GOOD MORNING, SAJA," Jeanette greeted me as I entered the cafeteria.

She came over, took me by the elbow, and ushered me to her office.

"Good morning," I answered, uncertain of what to expect. I wondered, *Was Mia there to confront me?*

Jeanette had always been sweet, but today her tone was more jovial than usual. I tried to muster some courage to tell her that I was not coming back to the cafeteria. It wasn't easy to stop, as I had grown fond of her for giving me the chance to help in the kitchen. In a way, I felt that I had betrayed her by throwing in the towel so easily.

"Mia's not coming today. She's not coming back," Jeanette announced, looking at me knowingly, as if she had witnessed what happened yesterday.

"Aha," was all I managed to utter.

"Okay, let's start," Jeanette said, patting my shoulder.

I nodded and went to back to fetch my apron.

WHEN I LEFT the cafeteria at the end of the day, a light rain was falling. I hadn't brought a rain jacket with me, since my plan had been to say goodbye to Jeanette and return to my barracks. It had never occurred to me that I would stay the whole day.

The cold wind blew the raindrops in a way that gave them the appearance of silver threads falling diagonally.

Today is a day of miracles, I thought while enjoying this little gift of nature. I was so absorbed by the weather that I missed the footsteps behind me. When I turned around to see who was approaching, it was too late. The blow floored me.

I fell on all fours and saw the familiar hat's brim pulled over his eyes.

A scream was choked in my throat.

"Sex," he hissed, as he slapped my face.

The metallic taste of my own blood filled my mouth as I rolled on the mud. Now the man dragged me by my arms as I kicked madly in a desperate attempt to disrupt his plans. He stumbled in the mud and paused for balance. I tried to rise from the ground but he pulled me down by my hair.

My mind commanded me to scream but not even a whisper came out of my mouth. He dragged me perpendicular to the path, along a corridor between the rows of barracks. Finally, a shout came from my throat, like an echo in a tunnel.

"Help!" I cried hysterically and kept screaming, searching for the knife I carried hidden on my waist.

"Bitch," he cried as he ran in the opposite direction.

Suddenly, I heard the sound of people running toward me. I kept shouting for help until they found me in a pit of mud, with torn clothes, holding the grill knife in one hand.

Chapter

12

NOW MORE THAN ever, I made it a habit to stop by the Red Cross office to check the bulletin board. I came twice a day to see if there was news regarding my case.

I have to leave this place as soon as possible became my motto.

The man with the hat was no longer a problem, since he had run away the same day he attacked me, as many had predicted he would.

The episode was now in the hands of the police, but I would always be in danger as long as I stayed in the camp as a widow. It was just a matter of time before another man would attempt the same act.

Everyone told me that most of the cases that were resolved within three months ended in deportation, but no time that had passed would guarantee that the authorities would grant me a residence permit, either. What if the police could not confirm my identity? I didn't even remember the last time when my number had appeared on the board, since I received the last letter from the Red Cross staff at the barracks. It didn't look good but I really wanted to keep my spirits high.

Today I went to check the board early—nothing new, of course. But after lunch, I went back to the board and this time, my number was there.

The staff handed me a white envelope with the words Immigration Service and the agency's logo. Now that I had the letter in hand, I did not dare open it.

I had been waiting so long for this. I finally stood at the crossroads that would define my future. I had no idea how many times I had dreamed about holding the letter. I knew exactly how I would feel, what I would say, and how I would react, but nothing compared with actually being in the moment.

I returned to the barracks but didn't go to my room. I just sat on a bench close to where I lived, holding the letter and wondering whether it was written in Danish or not. Anyway, I would not understand what it said. I felt a great sense of peace, with not a single trace of fear or anxiety. It was rather a breath of relief. No more uncertainty, regardless of the decision of the Immigration Service.

I approached my door, but the news that there had been a letter addressed to me arrived first. Some neighbors were already waiting for me at the entrance.

"Well?" they asked in chorus.

"I don't know; I haven't opened the letter yet," I said with a nervous smile.

"What are you waiting for?"

"I'm sure the letter is written in Danish," I said apologetically and noticed that the initial gleam in their eyes when they saw me, as they were hungry for good news, became a grimace of disappointment.

They had been there when the gypsy attacked me and had called the police, and we had all shared the misfortune of running away from our countries. So even though I would have preferred some privacy to read the letter and curse in solitude, if necessary, I decided to open it in front of them.

I tore open the envelope as they crowded around me. This time the letter was written in English.

Chapter

13

WE JUMPED, WE hugged, and we cried. People gave me their blessings in many different languages. Everyone celebrated the joy of my good fortune, as though it were theirs, a collective achievement, which also gave them hope.

"Bring me luck," said one of my neighbors, "put your right hand on my forehead."

When the others heard his request, they stood in line to make me do the same for them.

"I'VE HEARD THE news, you sweet thing," Jeanette said, spreading her arms to give me a hug, as I walked into the cafeteria the next morning.

"Yes," I said, weeping with joy for the second time.

"Count on me for a good word about you, if you need a reference," she offered.

I KEPT HELPING in the cafeteria until I received a letter from the municipality and an envelope from the police with certified copies of my diplomas from Red River College and the Paul Bocuse Institute for my records, which were in themselves another blessing, as these documents would smooth the way for me to find a job.

Apparently, the Immigration Service had been about to close my case, when the police faxed them my picture from the yearbook of Red River in Canada. That was how they were able to confirm my identity.

THE MUNICIPALITY OF Fredensborg assigned me a student apartment on the third floor of a building in Kokkedal, close to Egedal Church. When I opened the door, I felt as if I were at the entrance of my own palace. It was tiny but had all the essentials—a little kitchen, a living room, and a bathroom.

What more could a woman who had lost her past wish for? I had my privacy. I could see the playground, which was clean and empty, and a blue line far away that suggested it was Nivaa Bay.

Soon after I moved in, the municipality sent me a letter to attend a mandatory course in Danish for foreigners.

While attending the Danish classes, I also began to search for a job. My chances were not many, as I did not have an Internet connection in the apartment and the local library was only open on Tuesdays and Thursdays from 10:00 a.m. to 3:00 p.m., when I was supposed to be butt-down in the classroom. So I managed to use the computers from the Language Center until I found out about a much larger library with self-service and open hours up to 10:00 p.m.

During one of the breaks in the Danish course, I overheard a conversation about a Japanese restaurant that was hiring waiters. I asked for details and headed for the restaurant after class. It was only a half-hour trip, but despite the short ride, I appreciated how the landscape drastically changed as we approached the city.

When I got off the train, I realized that this was the same train station where Arumuka Navalar had left me when I had arrived in Copenhagen for the first time.

I remembered the arches at the exits, which had seemed pulled from a mosque, the red and white tiles, and the column with the clock where the agent left me.

I had stopped with a slight stumble as passengers rushed on their way to the bus stop. At that time, I had thought that those passengers at least had a destination. They had someone with whom to share the end of the day.

The same feeling struck me today, but this time I had a purpose, even though I had no one to meet me at the apartment, an apartment naked of the past, of memories. I didn't even have pictures of my family or Thani. By fleeing Sri Lanka, I had lost any tangible proof of my past.

Fortunately, the restaurant was not so far from the station. I followed the stream of people heading for the exit on Bernstorffsgade Street, from where I could see the amusement park. I felt the same thrill as the people riding the roller coaster, just by hearing their screams.

As my classmate had suggested, I went to the traffic light on the right, toward Tietgensgade Street. I walked about a hundred yards to the left until I spotted the glass facade with the restaurant's name on it in black lettering.

The place was crowded so I understood why they needed waiters. I had pictured the restaurant differently; I had thought of it as a more traditional sushi bar but it didn't disappoint me. The place created the impression of being huge, thanks to the glass facade. The furniture was simple but tasteful: long, light wooden tables with matching backless benches, an open kitchen to the right where the chef was flaming something in a frying pan, huge, white string lamps, and a bunch of young waiters in red t-shirts and black pants, taking orders.

The guy who met me at the entrance thought I was a customer. When I explained to him the reason for my visit, he said I should send an unsolicited application.

"Do you have references?" he asked when I was about to leave.

"Yes," I replied without thinking twice, hoping that Jeanette would keep her promise.

I did send an application but didn't expect much, since the entire team appeared way younger than me. To my surprise, I was invited to an interview and came out with a contract. I started doing ten-hour shifts a week; before long, I was taking orders in English and French. At first, I had no idea about Japanese cuisine. I took home a copy of the menu and prepared some of the recipes myself so I could better explain the difference between *ebi gyoza* and *ebi katsu*.

Chapter

14

I THOUGHT THAT waiting tables in a Japanese restaurant would be boring, especially after all my years working on *nouvelle cuisine*. I remembered the days at the Paul Bocuse Institute. My idea had been to acquire some knowledge to add an international twist to the Sri Lankan delicacies. Waiting tables at the Japanese eating place awoke the hope of starting my own restaurant. Who knew? Maybe I would learn a few tricks of Japanese cuisine I could apply to my *brinjals*.

One thing was certain: I didn't lose track of what the chef was doing in the kitchen.

GRADUALLY MY APARTMENT acquired some personality. It was a rough thing because I didn't have mementos of the past—no pictures, no inherited furniture from my elders, nothing. Not even a decent budget to buy stuff. But I was lucky to find a merry, lovely blue sofa bed in a secondhand furniture shop that gave life and color to my little place. I also added some flowers that could survive with little care. I would have loved to grow some orchids but they needed space and lots of water and were very expensive on this side of the world, so I bought a few *bellis* buds and a pair of *fuchsia* and *lantana* that I put by the only window.

MY TIME WAS split between the language school and the restaurant. The weekends were like rainy days, spent doing the laundry, cleaning the apartment, doing my assignments for the Danish class. The few friends I made were married. It never occurred to me to seek my compatriots in the camp as they considered me less worthy for being a widow and escaping Sri Lanka without a male family member. I guessed it was much worse outside. It was sad to come home to an empty place, where I only talked to the flowers and enjoyed the company of the books I borrowed from the library, so when the team leader at the restaurant offered me a few extra hours during the weekends, I decided to take them.

"Saja, would you take care of table six?" Michelle asked me.

"Sure! Are you about to leave?"

"Yes, and I'm about to miss the train," she explained on her way to grab her jacket.

"Go, I'll take care of it," I reassured her. I took my notepad and went to the table, where three adults were waiting.

"Welcome. Is this your first time?" I asked with a smile.

"No, we've been here before," replied the only woman at the table, and the two men nodded.

"Are you ready to order or do you want to try something new?"

"A *salmon ramen* for me, please," the woman said.

"A *yaki udon* for me," added the man sitting across from her.

"I'll go for a *yaki soba yasai*, please," said the other man, who was sitting next to the woman. That voice sounded familiar to me. I jotted down the numbers from the menu and looked up to notice that he, too, was observing me.

We held our glances for a few seconds; I was sure that he had also recognized me. It was the same man who had been present at my last Immigration Service interview, and I was racking my brain to remember his name. I studied the blond woman but she didn't seem the same person from the interview.

He watched me, yet when I was about to greet him, he quickly lowered his eyes.

Was he ashamed of knowing the waitress?

He didn't acknowledge me so I gathered that he was pretending he didn't know me. I decided to play safe.

"Something to drink?" I asked now, avoiding his eyes.

I took the orders and rushed to the kitchen.

"Louise?" I called the waitress who returned from the cash register.

"Saja, you won't believe it; the last customer left a miser's tip," she confided as she approached me.

"Any other table?" I asked, ignoring her remark.

"Nothin'," she gestured with her thumb down. "What, got somethin' for me?"

"Table six," I said, handing her the order.

"That's my girl," she responded with a hug.

"Okay, okay, and please don't let them wait."

"Send some more tables my way, okay?"

"I'll keep that in mind," I replied as I glanced at the glass wall to catch the reflection of the group of three. I didn't like the mood of despair that struck me.

"Why should I care if he pretends he doesn't know me?" I muttered through clenched teeth.

Chapter

15

"SAJA, AREN'T YOU going to take table three?" Michelle asked with a hint of irony, referring to the man who came every Sunday at the same time.

"Stop it," I hissed, pretending I was angry.

"Come on, Saja, he means business. Is this, what, the third, fourth time in a row?"

"Please, Michelle, stop it; he might hear you."

"Relax, dear, there's plenty of noise here, okay?"

Now everyone in the restaurant ribbed me good-naturedly about how his eyes were fixed on me.

At first, I hadn't remembered his name, so I checked the correspondence I kept from the refugee camp and found his name on one of the first letters, in connection with the attendees of the third interview. He had been the only man there so I was certain that he was Peter Frederiksen.

But I was totally confused by his behavior, as he pretended he didn't know me the first time he came. What was he doing here then?

He usually came, asked for table three if it was available, ordered the same *yaki soba yasai* without touching it, observed me—or so my colleagues said—and left.

To worsen matters, he told Katie, the waitress who had welcomed him the second time, that he would rather have *me* take his order.

Since then, he became known at the restaurant as the "Viking of Sri Lanka"; my colleagues didn't have any idea that I had known him from before I started at the restaurant. Otherwise, it would have been like adding more fuel to the fire of their mockery.

Peter managed very well for himself, I had to admit, since on one of his visits, he showed up with a rose with a long, thick stem and dark petals the color of a ripe cherry. Again he ordered *yaki soba yasai*, I presumed to justify his presence, as the dish came back to the kitchen untouched. About a half-hour later, Peter paid the bill and left the rose on the table.

Now everyone was wondering what I was waiting for, either to speak to the Viking or to make it clear that I wasn't interested.

I hadn't forgotten that Peter had pretended in front of his friends that he didn't know me, so I was uncertain. When my shift was over, I said goodbye to my colleagues, rolled the scarf around my neck, grabbed my jacket, and walked toward the Central Station.

When I reached the traffic light to turn right on Tietgensgade Street, Peter was standing at the corner with hunched shoulders, his chin tucked in the scarf, shivering with cold.

I stopped for a moment and observed him.

"Excuse me for what I did the other day," he said, almost guessing my thoughts.

"Excused, and thanks for the rose," I replied, reaching out to shake hands. "My name is Saja but I guess you already know that."

"Peter," he said. "Going to the station?"

I nodded.

"Do you mind if I walk with you?"

"Not at all."

He gave me a cheerful expression and lowered his head, perhaps fearful of revealing too much.

"I'm glad you finally got the residence permit," he whispered.

"Thank you."

I didn't know what to say. Those days in the refugee camp had been traumatic, so I also lowered my head.

"Not my problem but I'll say it anyway," he said sternly and stepped aside.

"Aha?"

"You have a lot of potential so don't stay there long," Peter explained, pointing toward the restaurant.

"Thank you," I replied, blushing. "This job is temporary. I plan to stay there until I finish the Danish course."

We walked the rest of the way in silence as the stunted sun of October hid behind clouds that seemed like a flock of sheep.

The Central Station filled with echoes, hurried footsteps coming and going, strolling musicians, and noise coming from the adjacent streets. Peter walked with me to platform one. I thanked him silently, as the place was almost deserted and being alone might have been dangerous. He said something but the clanking of the trains slowing down on the other platforms drowned out his words.

"Sorry, what did you say?"

"Nothing important," he said without bitterness.

My train arrived. It was red and sprayed all over, but at the train station, very little escaped the graffiti artist.

I thanked Peter again for the rose and stepped into the train. I stood by the door and waved at him as the train moved slowly away.

PETER WAS NOW coming to the restaurant almost every Sunday.

"Saja, the Viking is here," my colleagues would announce, happy that I had met someone.

He usually came when my shift was about to finish, and we sometimes walked through the amusement park or just strolled around holding hands.

"When are you going to invite me to eat something prepared by you?" he once asked between bites of churro with chocolate.

"Have you ever had specialties from Sri Lanka?"

"The closest are *samosas* of potatoes and peas," he answered with a shrug.

"They're related but not exactly the same."

"I'm vegetarian," he said apologetically.

"Really?"

"Yep."

"You mean ... are you vegan?"

"No, no, I eat dairy and eggs."

"What a coincidence," I said, smiling. "Well, in two weeks I have Sunday off. If you want, I can prepare something for you to taste."

"Deal," he agreed, sealing the pact with a smile.

WE ATE ON the sofa bed; I didn't have room for a proper table. I had bought wine glasses from a secondhand shop, but I forgot to buy candles, too. So I improvised with some banana-wick lamps like those we used in

Sri Lanka at weddings to ward off the evil eye.

Peter respected my reluctance to talk about my past. Instead, he told me all about his childhood and his hippie dad, who had allowed him to do whatever he wanted. They had enjoyed long walks on the shore during the summers, ate blueberries in September until these gave them indigestion, and consumed piles of pancakes with honey on top while his mom was taking shifts at the hospital.

He also told me that his father ran away with an American dancer. Peter missed him a lot but he couldn't hate his father, since he was the kind of person one couldn't be mad at. Never pushing, never in a hurry, never stressed.

"He was so relaxed that one summer we took Janis, the old Volkswagen Type2 orange van, for a long ride. Before long, we had to pull over, as poor Janis started to smoke. We managed to jump out, right before she caught fire. Dad took me by the hand as we walked away to sit on the edge of the road. He took a cigarette from his pocket and enjoyed it there. '"Well, I guess we have to walk,' was all he told me," Peter recalled, shaking his head with a smile.

"Dad was completely oblivious to duties of any kind; he was a free bird," Peter continued. "Mom, however, took his betrayal stoically. She never spoke ill of him but she didn't accept the little cottage he left, either. She let me keep it.

"In the beginning, I didn't know what to do with the cottage. I was only sixteen. The little house was very primitive but had the essentials for spending a couple of days in it. Dad managed to grow some potatoes and carrots. After he left, I went to clean up the place and found some bushes behind the greenhouse that didn't seem to have grown there by a whim of nature. The more I observed the plants, the more I became convinced this wasn't a case of life emerging from dead matter. By the way they stood aligned, they appeared more like the conscious effort of my dad's hand. The shrubs gave off a musky odor and had these long, pointy leaves with spiky edges, as if zigzag scissors had cropped them, and they spread out like the tale of a peacock. I asked around among my buddies. 'Awesome man, your old man was growing *cannabis,*'" he said, mimicking his best friend's gestures.

Peter shook his head while reliving the memories of his father. It was a very special moment, this Viking sitting on my sofa, opening his heart, allowing himself to be vulnerable, so I didn't dare break the spell.

"I seriously considered selling the cottage to close the chapter, but that place meant a lot to me because I spent happy moments of my childhood there. So that settled the issue," Peter explained.

"I'm glad I kept the cottage, because a few months after Dad ran away to America with the dancer, both died in a car accident. Mom took it badly; she never remarried and kept dressing in black. She is now retired and lives in Farum. She's still fresh enough to terrify the neighbors in her battle to maintain the alley clean and tidy, and she too pesters me to marry any woman other than Erica."

"What's the story with Erica?" I asked as we sipped the Belgian beer that Peter had brought for dinner.

"We remain friends," he confessed.

"She knows you're here today?"

"Erica knows everything about you."

I noticed Peter's discomfort while speaking about her, by the way he looked at the wall, and how he shook his leg stretched in front of him. As he scratched his head, I decided to change the subject.

"What do you do at the Immigration Service?"

"I'm a biologist but I've never worked in a lab. However, I have worked on projects for water purification in disaster areas. After a few years doing that, I became hungry for new challenges. Thanks to my international experience, and as I found out that I'm good at streamlining processes, I landed this position at IS."

"What kind of processes?" I wanted to know.

"We've been working on other alternatives to avoid delays in the processing of asylum applications."

"Do you like what you do?"

"I'm not that happy because we haven't achieved better results."

"Was that the reason you were present at the interview back then?"

"Sorry, I shouldn't be talking about those kinds of details."

"Fair enough," I replied. "Do you fancy some dessert?"

"What's on the menu?"

"Passion fruit ice cream garnished with sour cream."

"Sure," he said as he helped me carry the dishes to the kitchen.

Peter helped me clean up as we talked a lot about everything, mostly harmless topics, education, childhood, music, trips, and tastes. We kissed smoothly, softly, and deeply, as if we'd known each other for a long time. We weren't in a hurry as if we, in a sense, knew each other's scars. We finished the beers and laughed out loud the next morning, when we realized that we fell asleep completely dressed.

Chapter 17

PETER

"LONE, YOU WANTED to speak with me?" Peter asked as he poked his head into his boss' office.

"Yes, come in and close the door."

"What's happened?" he asked as Lone frowned at him.

"Sit down," she said, pointing to the chair in front of her desk.

The tone of her voice gave him a bad feeling, since Lone had always been jovial and they had maintained a good working relationship. Peter knew she wanted a report from him explaining the cause of the delays in processing the visa applications, and she knew all about why he was reluctant to put his name on that matter. *That must be it*, he thought.

"You know why you're here?" Lone asked, looking straight into his eyes.

"No idea," Peter confessed as he opened his arms in surrender.

"Do you remember the case of the woman from Sri Lanka?"

The question fell in the same way as if someone opened the door while one was sitting on the toilet.

"Which?" Peter managed to ask as Mads Lambeck stepped into the office.

He and Hagrid would have made an excellent duo, thought Peter as the giant greeted him with a brief nod and sat on the chair next to him.

"Peter, we have information that you are dating a refugee. Is it true?" Lone resumed.

"That's private," Peter said, crossing his arms.

"Peter, that would be private if the girl you're dating was not a refugee in one of the cases in which you were directly involved," Lone replied, putting her hands on the armrests of the chair, as if she was about to stand up.

"That case was already closed when we started dating, and that decision was made based on the data we collected. I have not ..."

"Peter," Mads interrupted, "we know how the decision was made. We know that all the rules were followed according to our SOP. The problem is that if the press finds out, they will speculate that you might, in some way, have tipped the balance in her favor. The key issue is that your relationship with her creates a conflict of interest because you're dating a refugee you knew while her case was pending. We can't afford that, period."

"Of course I see the conflict when you put it that way, but the truth is that Saja and I started dating long after she got her permit."

"Peter, we are willing to give you six months' salary plus two months' bonus due to your seniority," Lone announced, ignoring Peter's comment.

"This is absurd," Peter gasped, clutching his head.

"You don't want to know how we found out?"

"What difference does it make? We're not hiding," Peter snapped at her.

"It was none other than Erica," she revealed.

"Erica?" Peter repeated, unable to believe what Lone had just said.

"Yes, Erica."

"You mean, Erica, my ex?"

"No, Erykah Badu," said Lone impatiently. "Peter, you are too naive."

"But I thought she was my friend," he said as he dropped farther back on the chair.

"Peter, in a way she is, as she wasn't after you; she wanted Saja's case reopened to kick her out of the country. Erica is anything but your friend." Lone paused. "That anaconda of an ex of yours told us that if we didn't do something about it, she would go to the newspapers with the story."

Peter liked the comparison Lone had made with the snake. He even gave her a half-smile. Not because he thought it was funny, but because he saw the irony as Lone used Erica to mask the softness of her own character.

"So you delivered me instead?"

None of them answered.

"Accept the offer and take a break," Mads suggested.

Peter observed the two of them, as he felt being in the presence of two strangers. He had worked with them for the last six years and now all was lost. They had let him down. Peter was disappointed to see them fall on their knees before the intrigues of a woman who clearly felt scorned.

What else could explain why Erica had come here with the story?

To some extent, Peter understood that they were following the policy of avoiding scandal at all costs. Cases from the recent past had illustrated why neither of them would want to be near the least thing with a whiff of scandal.

The Tamils' incident that had led to the prime minister's resignation back in the eighties and the scandal of 2008, which involved cases of frontline staff who simply refused to accept residence application forms of foreign spouses brought by Danish citizens, confirmed that neither Lone nor the big man would put their hands into the fire to stand by Peter.

Suddenly, Peter felt the urge for fresh air, to just run away from this meeting. He shuddered to see how Erica had manipulated these two puppets. He glanced around once again. How many times had they been in the same office? He didn't remember and it really didn't matter anymore. When Peter stood up, he realized that he was no longer listening to whatever Lone was saying. He headed toward the door and exited the office without slamming the door.

He walked toward one of the quiet rooms and grabbed his mobile phone as he closed the glass door. He took the right name from the recent phone calls' list and dialed.

Erica took the call almost immediately, as if she was expecting him to call.

"You piece of shit! If I ever hear from you, I swear I'll tell everyone about what happened in Sardinia. You hear me?" he muttered as he felt his heart pumping up his tonsils when he hung up.

Erica, Erica, Peter thought, shaking his head.

He had told her all about Saja because after all, he himself ended up hearing about the romantic encounters Erica had with other men. The only difference was that to Peter, Saja wasn't a mere one-night stand, and he had believed that Erica was his friend.

What resulted, to his surprise, was that she had denounced him out of spite. He also realized that Erica was not only mad at him, but also wanted a piece of Saja. *But why?,* he wondered as he paced the floor, stopping short as he remembered something Saja mentioned on the day of the interview.

He laughed aloud. "There's your answer, Peter!"

"Not all who enter finish the course," Saja had said and he remembered how this little unwitting sentence had slashed Erica as a reminder that she herself had not made it to the end of the training in Lyon.

What was Erica thinking? That I would take her back? Just picturing the possibility made his skin crawl.

Thanks to Google, Peter had been spared a future bearing the mark of Erica's infidelities.

Yes, Erica was really beautiful. Her body was a delicacy and her carnal appetite was impossible to quench.

"I'm attending a gourmet workshop," Erica had announced when they still lived together, and both decided to plan it so that she would fly to Sardinia. Peter fancied long strolls across Monte d'Accordi, holding hands with her, but not this time, as he had to take the train to Aarhus instead, for three weeks of training that he had been putting off.

When he returned to the apartment, Erica was out but her bag was on the edge of the bed.

She should be near, Peter thought.

He had been unpacking his stuff when her bag fell on the floor. His quick reflexes caught the bag in midair, but a key ring and a box flew out of it. He picked up both things from the floor. The name on the package struck him: *Doxycycline*. His heart was pumping and some part of him didn't want to believe it. He wasn't completely sure, but a bell kept ringing in his head, after his many years as a biologist.

Erica wasn't home so Peter asked Google.

Peter knew that one uses doxycycline to treat a number of infections. A list of bacteria and diseases had appeared on the screen of his old PC: *rickettsia, brucellosis, E. coli*, but his heart skipped a beat when the words *Neisseria gonorrhoeae* and *Chlamydia trachomatis* appeared on the list, confirming his fears. He closed his eyes, as he got the impression that both terms had flashed in front of him. The skin on his face felt dry and his hands went numb. He had placed the box next to her bag, packed his stuff back into the carry-on luggage, and left the apartment.

Peter never mentioned the incident to anyone. He simply packed up and broke the engagement. Apparently, the move had shaken the carpet in Erica's life to such an extent that she had kept calling until Peter gave up and talked to her again.

At no time did they ever talk about the pills, nor did they share the same bed again. They went out for beers and drank a lot, and everyone took for granted that they would be back together. Their assumptions amused Peter, realizing how little they knew him. As a couple, he and Erica were finished and that was irreversible.

Saja had attracted him with her strength, as he had never seen anyone standing up for herself as she had done in the interview. Saja had guts when she asked Vinnie if she thought that she came from a beach resort.

From his point of view, there was no comparison between her and Erica. Saja had a backbone, principles, and a clear vision of what she wanted in life. Furthermore, she could afford to write volumes about the word "loyalty," which made her an exquisite woman.

Chapter

18

PETER

AFTER THE MEETING with Lone and Mads Lambeck, Peter went to his desk to pick up the few things he would take with him. Somebody said something but he didn't really listen. Peter would have preferred to use a box to carry all his stuff, but he gave up on the idea because he didn't want to ask the receptionist. This would have led to questions he didn't want to answer.

At his desk, he opened the upper drawer, where he found a yellow plastic bag. He took a brief look at the desk and smiled at the amount of junk he had collected all these years, as he spotted a coffee jar with the Immigration Service (IS) logo, which he had used as pencil holder.

Out, he thought.

Then he looked around and saw the bib numbers of the last three DHL relay races in which he had participated on behalf of the IS, pinned up on a corkboard. He pulled them down and tossed them into the trash can.

Someone else can take care of it, he thought as he grabbed all the Post-its stuck around the computer screen. He made a ball of them and threw them out, too.

Peter removed a yellowish picture of his dad sleeping on the grass, with an unbuttoned shirt and a newspaper over his chest, taken at the Woodstock festival. He also removed the photos of himself that were laid under the clear desk mat, from his time as a volunteer in Africa. He

71

put them carefully into the bag.

"No way in hell I'll bring those with me. Lone, you can sit on those," he muttered as he looked at two cacti sharing the same wavy white pot, one pale green with puffy leaves, like an artichoke, and the other like a cucumber topped with a yellow mass, pretty much like a miniature pumpkin. They had been a present from Lone in an attempt to humanize the desktop of her "favorite employee," as she had put it.

They all knew that a head would roll today, thought Peter, as he took his phone and the bag with the photos and quietly walked down the suspiciously empty hall.

"SAJA, YOU ARE obsessed with kids; you just want children. How can you think of starting a family when we don't have economic stability?"

Her laughs sounded like the beads of a broken necklace spreading all over the floor, when Peter told her. To her, it was funny that he made it sound like an accusation, as if wanting children were something shameful.

"So you think I'm going too fast?" she asked, knowing the answer.

"Saja, I lost my job three months ago, I keep sending job applications everywhere, and I don't even get acknowledgment of receipt. How on earth am I going to start a family?"

"Peter, there is always going to be a bump on the road—unemployment, career, lack of money, lack of time, we are too young or we are too old for that, political instability ... Peter, do you think that no children were born during Sri Lanka's civil war? The ideal situation doesn't exist," she said, clasping her fingers in a theatrical gesture.

"Saja, I won't have children if I don't have a job," he announced, lowering his head.

"So you are sure that when you find another job, you won't lose it?"

He didn't answer and went to the kitchen instead. He grabbed a glass and poured water into it.

"I respect your not wanting to have children, so there is no point in staying together," Saja said as she picked up her scarf and jacket from the back of a chair.

"Saja, we just submitted the application for the restaurant project. If

72

they approve it, you won't have time to babysit anyway."

"It isn't likely that they will grant us the money. You see? Pessimism is contagious," she replied before leaving his apartment.

Chapter

19

"YOU GOT IT," I heard someone saying behind me.

This was one of those days when almost everything had gone wrong: cranky customers who couldn't decide what to order, someone who returned a firecracker steak because it was cold and sent it back again because it had too much chili on it, and bad tippers. On top of that, there was a little drama when a guest picked the wrong waitress to air her frustration. The Visa she was trying to use to pay for the meal had been rejected three times.

"These waiters ... Don't you know how to use that machine?" the woman hissed.

"Ma'am, there's nothing wrong with the machine," Michelle said as she went to the cash register, took out a pair of scissors and cut the credit card in front of the woman.

Now what, I thought, as I turned around to find a slightly thinner version of Peter standing in front of me.

"Why don't you take my calls?" he asked.

It was a question but it sounded more like a plea.

It was wonderful to see him again but something in my mind kept saying, *Saja, don't get too excited.*

"Sorry, what did you say?" I felt as though my heart was crawling up my throat.

"Why don't you call me back?"

"I was hurt," I confessed as I looked around, well aware that Michelle and Katie were watching us, smiling and giggling from the kitchen. I cherished them both; the place was about to fall down yet they managed to keep up their good spirits.

"Saja, we have the money for the project. You won," he told me with an earnest smile.

"No, Peter, *you* won. It would have been fun to do it together with you. To me, it was a joint dream but as things stand, it's different now," I said, lowering my head, unable to hold his gaze.

"Saja, I want to be part of it."

"Peter, we're not dating anymore. I want a man who wants to start a family."

"Saja, I'm here."

"You're here for the project."

"I'm here for both."

THE RESTAURANT PROJECT had come to life from a comment I made to Peter on a Friday over a couple of Trappist beers.

"It saddens me, the piles of good food we throw away at the restaurant."

Peter scratched his head. "Have you ever seen the containers at the supermarkets?"

"Yes. Most of the vegetables are not even rotting; they just have a couple of bruises."

"I read the other day on the newspaper about a jerk from a supermarket who took a leak into the containers and left a note to let the dumpster divers know."

"Think of how many homeless people would benefit from the discarded food," I reflected.

"There you have material for a project," Peter said, his eyes wide open.

"Are you kidding?"

"Why not? Imagine the good PR: private organizations funding a cause for the homeless," Peter declared, jumping up from the sofa, arms spread like a pop singer on the spotlight.

WHEN WE WENT into details, just to have an idea of what it meant to open a restaurant, I realized that the project was doomed to die. It was too ambitious, as my vision was that of a nonprofit restaurant, a place where the homeless would come to have a meal.

The raw materials would come from the supermarket chains and untouched food from the canteens of private companies, which meant that we would have to find a way to pick up the stuff. This posed a challenge with regard to logistics and transportation. We needed a place for the restaurant, an approved kitchen and staff, and surely a bunch of volunteers. But as far as Peter was concerned, the more hurdles in the way, the more excited he became.

THANKS TO PETER'S tireless lobbying, plenty of companies were willing to sponsor the idea. Once word spread, help came disguised in the most amazing ways and at different stages. Jeanette from the refugee camp came to inspect the kitchen to make sure the authorities wouldn't find issues in the premises, which would delay the approval. Michelle and Katie offered to help a couple of hours every second week. Peter's mom had contact with a rug weaver who donated three lovely Wayuu rugs to decorate the place, and some regulars volunteered to do the dishes in exchange for a free meal.

Hope, our restaurant, was always packed, primarily with homeless people, but also with paying customers who came just to support us. It seemed that the idea had inspired others; rumor had it that a group of youngsters was doing something similar. They charged for the food, though the profits were used to fund charitable projects.

I WOKE UP before the alarm clock rang. I could hear Peter's breathing next to me. I loved watching him asleep, abandoned and peaceful. It often reminded me of something he told me long ago.

"Peter, I know you like to sleep on your right side. I don't mind looking at your back," I said once after a long day at work when we were about to go to bed.

"No," he said with a tired smile. "I want you to be the last image of the day." He laid his head on the pillow and finally drifted off to sleep.

I looked around us in the darkness. There was a heap of clean clothes on the chair next to the dresser. One of the drawers was half-open, revealing a jumble of socks and underwear. I spotted how Peter's shoes piled up like ostrich eggs in the corner. Yes, we lived in a complete mess, as we spent the whole day at the restaurant, which left little room for house cleaning. We came home every night physically demolished but with fulfilled hearts.

A leaden light flowed gently through the cracks in the blinds. I stood on tiptoe and went straight to the bathroom, locking the door behind me so the light wouldn't disturb Peter's sleep.

I opened the drawer and pulled out the pregnancy test kit. I removed the testing stick from the wrapper, sat on the toilet, and took care of wetting the device as I peed over it. I felt the warmth of the fluid running through my fingers, and a mild stench of ammonia drifted out. When I finished, I put the kit on the edge of the washbasin. I took a shower to allow time for the test to do its job. When I finished, I used a couple of minutes with the towel, drying my locks of hair that almost covered my back. I applied body butter and two rounds of deodorant; I also dabbed a few drops of UMAMI perfume behind each ear. Peter gave me the sandalwood fragrance, as he wanted me to wear something with a Sri Lankan scent.

I realized that I was deliberately doing all this because I was scared of the results, scared of my age, and how the possibility of having children was fading away. I was terrified of the hundreds of negatives I had been getting since the times in Sri Lanka.

I let out a sob and took hold of the kit. My heart was now beating up my throat, when I spotted a sharp, thick fuchsia line on each side of the display screen. I felt I couldn't breathe, as the tears rolled down and I was unable to control them. I stayed there, sitting on the toilet, smiling with my eyes closed, enjoying the sensation of knowing that soon I'd have a little life throbbing in my belly. I tried to remember the lullabies my *amma* sang for me when I was little. Nothing came from that distant past. Instead, like a spark in the darkness, Tagore's poem came to me, whole:

A Better World

My life when young was like a flower
—a flower that loosens a petal or two from her abundance and never feels the loss
when the spring breeze comes to beg at her door.

Now at the end of youth my life is like a fruit, having nothing to spare, and
waiting to offer herself completely with her full burden of sweetness.

Yonna

Chapter

20

I WAS A WAYUU. That was how we said *person* in my tongue. We were called "the godless," the children of the rain, people of the sun. Some might say that we too were worthy of death, and although I'd died more than once, that was not what my story was about.

I was born during a downpour that opened cracks in the ground while other members of my clan danced the *yonna* to thank *Mareygua*, the Creator of the world and the bringer of *juya*, our word for rain. I belonged to the Epieyu caste, symbolized by the vulture—not only *Mareygua's* messenger, but also the carrier of the essence of the dead to the afterlife.

My mom, like any good *piache*, could unravel dreams. She could also walk in and out of the dead's world, heal diseases, and remain grateful through it all. Everyone danced the *yonna* to express gratitude for the rain. Since the dance symbolized the power struggle between men and women, my mother decided to call me Yonna.

My grandmother smelled like lemongrass and was a *piache*, my *piache*. She taught me how to knit, long before the seclusion at puberty. She once told me that when I was only three years old, I started weaving. "Little child! *Walekerü* tells you its secrets," she exclaimed at the sight of me playing with the needles and fabric, as her sunburned face transformed into the shell of a wrinkled passion fruit. I felt more Wayuu with each praise.

In my clan, the women wove, cooked, cared for the children, and washed the dead. The men fished and herded the goats. To us, the Wayuu people, nothing was more important than the burials and the seclusion.

To the Wayuu people, when a girl bled for the first time, she was ready to start a family, so she stayed in a dark room with her granny, who sang songs and told her stories; to take away bad habits, her granny also cut the girl's hair until it was fully shaved. The girl learned to weave during this time, and her granny washed her body at dawn with water from *juya* while the rest of the family was asleep.

After the seclusion, the girl was a *majayut* and therefore ready to receive the seed of man and bear his children. My people celebrated this by dancing the *yonna*. Men drank *chirrinchi* and ate grilled goat meat on the ever-burning campfire. Without a fire, there was no life; the house filled with ghosts and became a dead place.

All of my family members—my mom, my *piache* granny, my dad, and my eight brothers—perished during a *chicha maya*, the party the Wayuu threw to celebrate the end of my seclusion. I heard it was because of an offense against the Uriana clan that not even the babbler, a mediator, could resolve.

A whistle-blower from my clan, enraged because the Urianas took his trafficking business, had told the police the exact location of smuggled gas barrels the Urianas were about to transport to Colombia through the path of the trails. The police stopped the operation with the hope of getting money from the Urianas in return for turning a blind eye. As they never saw a single coin from the Urianas, they had no other choice but to do their job and seize the barrels. In response, the Urianas slaughtered my family with machetes for the offense.

Mareygua, our word for God, had other plans for me. I escaped from the same fate as the rest of my family only because I went to pee behind the house at the base of a banana tree. That was the first time I stopped feeling like a Wayuu.

The brawl with the Urianas left eighteen corpses from both families scattered all over, and the police came to inquire. The agents respectfully left the maimed parts as found, since only Wayuu women were allowed to touch the dead.

Instead, the police officers touched me.

The oldest officer was the least evil. His pockmarked face seemed much older than my *piache*'s. A few strands of greasy hair ran over his polished skull from one temple to the other, and the button of his shirt opened right over his prominent belly. As far as he was concerned, it was enough just to watch me. He drank his brandy and made me dance naked at gunpoint while he smoked a cigar.

I must have had some *piache* blood in my veins because at every onslaught of the agents, I learned to leave my own body. I became *Yeye*, a rag doll my granny knitted for me, in order to stop feeling pain and fear. I clearly saw my granny coming down to earth and gently joining my palms while she whispered lullabies in *Wayuunaki* to make me sleep, just as she did when I was little. I spent countless nights listening to the voice of my *piache* chanting, "It's over, it's over."

Unable to find joy in my body and tired of the smell of my vomit all over the place, the agents took me to some food stalls by the roadside in Paraguaipoa, opened the door of the jeep, and without much ceremony, ordered:

"Get off!"

Chapter

21

MY GRANNY WAS always with me, and with us was *walekerü*, the spider, the master weaver. I started weaving hammocks, hats, and sandals for *la señora* Meche, a woman who sold crafts at a small roadside stall, often to distributors in Maracaibo. They would drive the entire way to pick up the goods and resell them for a small fortune at luxury hotels. *La señora* forbade me from leaving, and my glee at her order surprised her. In return, she let me sleep in the back shop and paid me with three plates of food a day.

The only bad thing was Tomás, her nephew. He eyed me the same way as the police officers did, but *la señora* Meche didn't lose sight of him. Tomás did manage a couple of times to dodge her surveillance and greet me with a slap on the butt. The last time he tried, it caused a fit of vomiting in me, which splattered across his clothes. After that, he didn't dare approach me, although I did catch him watching me, waiting for another chance. I knew that sooner or later I would have to leave the stall.

One day, *la señora* Meche left me in charge of the stall for a couple of hours while she left to buy yarn for some commissioned hammocks. I was in the back shop, finishing the ground of a carpet, when I heard the sound of footsteps. I wasn't sure whether it was here or some place outside, as the deafening sound of the trucks' blaring horns at all times could drive you crazy.

"Hello?" a woman asked. Once again, a feeling of nausea started to build up in my stomach. I listened carefully to make sure that the person outside was alone.

"Hello," I replied, not daring to show myself.

"May I speak to *la señora* Meche?"

"She's away but she'll be back soon. Would you like to wait for her?" She answered but a truck drove by, muffling all that she said.

"I'm sorry, I couldn't hear you."

"How long ago was that?" she repeated.

"A couple of hours ago. It's odd she's not here yet," I insisted.

"And you help her with the sales?"

"No, I'm a weaver," I peeked around now that I was sure no one was with her. I saw a white woman—an *alijuuna*, a foreigner—wearing light linen clothes. Gold necklaces and bracelets adorned her neck and arms, and she protected her face with a straw hat. Her pale blue eyes were all over the place.

"You made all this?" she asked as she walked toward me. The faint fragrance of lemon came from her. I stepped back, nodding. She spoke Spanish but wasn't a native.

"Would you like some coffee?" I dared to ask.

"No, thanks, with this heat ..." she trailed off, fanning her face with one hand. "Would you show me what you're weaving?"

Now that I was closer, I realized her scent wasn't lemon but lemongrass. *The alijuuna smells clean,* I thought.

"Please, come here and I'll show you."

Upon entering, she fixed her eyes on the half-completed carpet I had been working on when she arrived. After examining the piece, the woman gasped, "How strange."

"Strange how?" I stammered. *La señora* Meche had a strict policy of not arguing with the customers.

"You're weaving a rug in blue. I don't remember seeing Wayuu carpets with blue backgrounds. Is it a custom?" she asked as she touched the piece, examining it closely.

"Yes, but it's my granny's, my *piache*," I said, assuming she understood the meaning. "She whispers the patterns to me and I weave them on the carpet."

86

"What is it? It resembles a blue sun."

"It's a star covering the sun."

"You mean an eclipse," the foreigner corrected.

"What is an eclipse?"

"A star blotting out the sun," she said with a smile.

"Do you like that carpet?" *La señora* Meche asked behind us. We both turned around to see her. She had just arrived, laden with bags of yarn. Tomás was standing by her side, holding the rest of the bags.

"I'll hire her," the *alijuuna* said.

"This is a custom carpet but I'm sure Yonna can weave another one just like it if you want. Isn't that right, Yonna?"

"I'm talking about the girl. Ask whatever you want for her."

"Yonna?" *la señora* Meche questioned, dropping the bags on the floor. "Yes."

Now the *alijuuna* talked to me, completely ignoring *la señora* Meche standing there. "If you want to, you can work for me, making your own money. You will learn to read and write, and you'll have your own bedroom. What do you say?"

"I can't let you hire her," *la señora* Meche interrupted. "She works for me but she can weave all the carpets you want."

Tomás was about to say something but *la señora* Meche commanded silence. I realized that she was using an unknown tone with the woman; she spoke carefully, as if measuring each word. Perhaps there was even a hint of fear in her voice.

"I'm not buying the girl. I'm buying her freedom," the woman said.

"I can't; she's the only weaver I have."

"That's why I would like to pay compensation."

"I can't," *la señora* Meche repeated, now shaking her head. "Yonna, go back."

"No problem. I can call the *polizei* and tell them that you're holding this girl in slavery conditions," said the *alijuuna,* her arms crossed. "You'll lose the weaver and the compensation."

The *alijuuna* was right. It wasn't that the police would be interested in an Indian girl like me, but if the complaint came from a white woman with money, the situation would become completely different.

"And why are you so interested in her?" *la señora* Meche asked with a hint of sarcasm.

"I gather she's your slave."

"She's got food and shelter."

"How much do you pay her for the carpets? Does she go to school? Is this what you call a shelter?" the woman inquired, spinning around.

"If she's forced to go to school, when is she going to weave the carpets people like *you* resell?" *la señora* Meche retorted.

There was a heavy silence. I did not dare move from my spot.

"What are you doing? Go to the back," *la señora* Meche cried.

I didn't move. For the first time, I saw my boss for who she really was. The flannel she wore was tight and you could notice the outline of two rolls of fat on either side of her hips. All of what was missing on her flat buttocks was concentrated in her chest. The olive green pants rolled up to her knees, like the camouflage pants worn by the military, didn't help improve her appearance. At least two fingers' width of dark roots gave away that her hair wasn't blonde.

"The girl will come with me unless she does not want to," the foreigner announced, fiddling with her jewelry. She opened her bag, pulled out a wad of cash, and laid it on the half-done carpet. "There! Now you have enough money to cover the cost of the stall and everything in it. And if I catch you near the hotel, I'll report you to the *polizei*."

"*Policía*, not *polizei*," *la señora* Meche corrected, as though she herself spoke Spanish perfectly. The *alijuuna* ignored the remark. She took my hand and pulled me out of the stall.

I didn't resist. I was terrified of Tomás and was already seriously thinking of running away. Barefoot, I briskly followed her to a metallic gray car parked a few meters ahead. She opened the passenger door and told me to get in. Like a robot, I followed her command. She opened the driver's side door, took her hat off, and threw it to the back seat, revealing her silver hair tied in a ponytail. From time to time, she glanced back at the stall we'd left behind, but no one came after us. She started the engine and a breath of cold air gave me goose bumps.

"Don't worry, it's air-conditioning." She turned up the temperature as she pointed to the black holes on the dashboard.

I nodded.

"By the way, my name is Dorothea Weiss but call me Thea," she said, putting the car in gear before we drove away at full speed.

Chapter

22

THEA KEPT HER promise. I worked for her and earned my own money. I also learned to read and write, and I slept on my own bed in my own bedroom. What she never said was that I also became master of my own destiny.

Thea lived in a colorful house in a neighborhood named after Santa Lucia's Church (a Gothic structure painted blue), where the houses were strung out in a long row. Despite having enough money to live in an upscale neighborhood, Thea chose this house; for a single woman, it was better to live in a place that was not too isolated.

Thea brought me there to live under her protection. I was struck by the contrast between the facade and the interior. Outside, the house was like all the others on the block, but inside were things I had never seen before. I guess Thea had decided to surround herself with elements of her homeland.

Nobody would have thought to put a sink on a leather trunk with many little doors, unless that person was named Thea Weiss. I carefully opened the doors, afraid of letting out hidden ghosts.

Thea smiled when I asked her what was the thing with tiger paws in the middle of the bathroom.

"It's a bathtub," she explained with her German accent. "You put water in it and lie down for a while."

"You don't drown?"

"*Nein,* only if you are careless. You just sit and enjoy the hot bath. This is very common in Europe, especially when the weather is cold."

"Yes, but it's not cold here. Only in that car of yours," I replied with a smile.

"Just wait until you try it; you'll love it," she assured me.

The kitchen was of inconceivable luxury to someone like me who only knew the campfire. Rustic cabinets fitted on the walls treasured a vast amount of dishes, pans, and pots of all sizes. Thea explained to me that it was the German country style. I couldn't understand why there were dishes hanging on the living room back wall when they should be in the kitchen, or why the bedroom windows were covered with heavy rugs as though it were a seclusion area.

I spent the first few nights lying on the floor of my new bedroom since I couldn't familiarize myself with the bed. The mattress was so soft that I was convinced it would swallow me once I lay down.

I wondered why she was living alone with no husband or children in Maracaibo. I tried to figure out how she ended up in this part of the world; surely, it was much different from where she came from. I didn't dare ask, though, and it turned out that I didn't need to. I guess these questions were painted on my face. She told me her story one day over a cup of coffee.

"In 1969, I arrived in Maracaibo. I came to this hot land, following Gualtiero Moretti—a beautiful, Italian opera singer who wanted to travel the world. We saw each other a few times and that was all it took to fall in love. After a couple of kisses, I knew I had to follow him to the end of the world if necessary. So when he asked me to come with him, I didn't think twice. I filled a leather suitcase with what I could and ran away with him. We were both twenty.

"Gualtiero Moretti thought that as soon as he set foot in Maracaibo, the audience would fall at his feet, asking for more *bel canto* melodies. It did not occur to him that on this side of the world, people preferred *joropos* over a yelling Italian.

"He tried his hand among the exquisite circles of that time's society. His new friends attended the few performances Gualtiero held at the Baralt Theater, more out of solidarity than real interest in opera. After a few months, the novelty of the Italian singer and his German girlfriend wore off, and they forgot all about us.

"The little money we had started to dwindle and I tried my hand at all of the trades taught in my native Hamburg. I ended up making jams, cakes, and sausages sold at rock-bottom prices that won immediate acceptance. I expanded the business into crafts, embroidering tablecloths and making bobbin lace.

"But Gualtiero ended up mired in a slump. He simply could not conceive that his destiny was to end up as a salesman after so many years of dedication to music. The more my business prospered, the deeper he sank into depression.

"Wanting to lift his mood, I bought him a record player so that he could find comfort in listening to opera while I ran around Maracaibo selling my goods. The enthusiasm that pushed us to travel to Maracaibo vanished within a few years but I still nourished the hope that he would ask me to marry him. When he never did, I knelt and proposed.

"Gualtiero took it badly. He thought I was mocking his misery and withdrew himself even more. He drank all the time and gave no rest to the record player. He stopped going out, eating, or seeing his old group of friends who vainly tried to do their best to cheer him up.

"'This land of savages does not understand my art,' he used to say. He became sullen and distrustful, and even hinted on more than one occasion that I was plotting to poison him.

"Soon after, he ended his own misery. I found him lying on the floor with open veins as Giuseppe Verdi was blaring in the living room," she said, pursing her lips in an attempt to repress her tears.

"Why didn't you go back to your country?" I wondered.

"Gualtiero was the reason I left everything in Germany. The possibility of returning to my homeland was out of the question, and it was he with whom I wanted to have children. Many laughed when they heard me say that never again would I have another man, but I think I earned their respect as time passed, and I kept my promise. I decided to stay here in Maracaibo and never fail to lay flowers on his grave every Sunday."

I got the sensation that it was the first time Thea had talked about these things. She wept quietly; I didn't know how to comfort her. I had learned the hard way to swallow my own tears.

Thea confessed that when she saw me at the stall with *la señora* Meche, she felt the urge to provide me with everything life had denied me. She also told me that she had the uncanny perception that I was the daughter she never had, and when she offered to buy me, it was only because she wouldn't have left if I didn't come with her.

"*Liebe* Yonna, tell me your story," Thea requested tearfully.

"My story?" I asked, startled, realizing that no one except my own family had ever been interested in my life.

"Yes."

I told her my story and she wept again.

Thea wanted to teach me all kinds of stuff so she undertook the task of helping me learn German. My only talent, though, was my ability to weave carpets, match colors, and depict on fabric the images my *piache* whispered to me during my dreams.

When Thea realized my lack of progress, coupled with how little practical utility such an enterprise really had, she ended up nurturing me with other *alijuuna* arts. With each new thing I learned, I felt what it was like being a real Wayuu—our word for person.

Chapter

23

THEA WAS THE owner of Dorotea's Craft Corner, a small shop located in one of the corners of a lavish hotel on El Milagro Avenue. This shop was a far cry from the dusty stall of *la señora* Meche. No traffic noise and the floor was carpeted in pale brown so you couldn't hear your own footsteps. At the center of the room was a rustic wooden table where Thea showcased handcrafted woolen bags, jars of honey and jam, neatly folded blankets, brightly colored animals carved into wood, and all kinds of local crafts. In one of the corners hung a gorgeous handwoven Wayuu hammock, while Wayuu carpets were piled in the opposite corner.

I asked Thea why she took the "h" out of her name on the shop sign.

"Just to give the business a more local name," she replied with a shrug.

She remodeled her own office with an *anülü*, which means loom among my people, so I could concentrate on my rugs and mats. Thanks to *Mareygua*, our God, Thea never demanded what I should weave. She didn't want to break the promise she made the day I escaped from *la señora* Meche's claws. It wasn't necessary, though, since we managed to sell every single piece I wove.

With time, word spread among the tourists about *Yonna's rugs*, so much so that we hardly managed to fill all the orders. At times, I wished I had an extra pair of hands to help.

"Yonna, I think we need an extra weaver. What do you think?" she asked me over a cup of coffee after a particularly long workday.

"Agreed," I said with a smile.

"Are you serious?" Thea sounded surprised.

"Yes, really. For some time now, I've been thinking that we need another weaver."

"Why didn't you tell me?"

"I didn't want to take advantage of your generosity," I said, unable to meet her eyes.

"After twelve years of living here and working for me, you feel you can't take advantage of my generosity? I have two candidates lined up. I'm sure it's going to work out."

Twelve years had indeed passed. I learned to lie in bed and fathom the meaning of sleeping all night. I caught on to reading and writing. Thea taught me how to use the cutlery, and I enjoyed long, hot baths. Perhaps most providentially, my *piache* went to *Jepira*, where the dead rest in peace.

The one thing I never did was to attend school. Thea tried to convince me but the sight of so many people coming in and out of the gates would always cause me to panic and run back to the house on El Milagro Avenue.

The craft shop was different; I was on my own, working with the loom, while Thea took care of sales.

Thea hired two Wayuu sisters from the *Zapuana* clan, whose animal is the curlew. I found it a good omen because *Zapuana* brought rain to our dry lands. Our plan went off perfectly. They already knew how to weave, were curious about my technique, and worked as hard as Thea and me.

Early one morning, Thea drove with me to the shop. While the *Zapuanas* wove my designs, I played with new materials and created new patterns. That was how I came up with the idea of carpets with silk threads, twisted strands of wool, and satin pieces that went on to become very popular.

The challenge was when Thea was away restocking raw materials for us, since that meant I had to stay at the front desk to take care of the customers. I hated the presence of strangers. To relax, I busied myself rearranging the goods.

I was on all fours when a customer came in.

"Hello," said the voice of a man, clearly an *alijuuna*.

"Hello," I replied on my knees.

From where I was, I could watch him move around the shop, trying to find who responded. When he did, he stopped short and looked at me straight in the eye for what I felt must have been hours. The sensation of ice cubes ran in my stomach, but something about his hazel eyes made me hold his gaze. I took a deep breath and held the air in my lungs for a few moments.

"May I help you?" I managed to ask, feeling a blush heating my cheeks.

He pointed with his thumb toward some object behind him without uttering a word. I tried to see what he was pointing at.

"The bag," he said. The "the" sounded long, as though he was having a hard time letting the words out.

"Ahh, that bag?" I pointed to a table covered with woven bags in various shades of brown.

"People love them. Do you want to buy one of those? I can wrap it as a gift."

"Yes, please. It's a present for my mother," he explained.

"Right away." I picked out some wrapping paper and began preparing the gift. My hands shook, causing me to rip the paper on my first try. I dropped the scissors a couple of times. It seemed that the more I felt the man's scrutiny, the clumsier I became.

"Let me help you with that," he offered, our fingers grazing as he reached forward. His touch was like an electric shock and I pulled my hand back on reflex.

"I think I can handle it," I said, but he insisted.

I took a deep breath and focused all my attention on wrapping the bag. Our fingers touched again and my cheeks lit up like a burner. I handed the present over to him, but as I turned, ready to run back to the safety of the loom, he called my attention.

"Aren't you going to charge me for the gift?" He appeared surprised.

"Oh yes, of course," I laughed nervously and took his money.

I heard him laugh, too. When I raised my face, his eyes fixed on mine.

"I'd better return to the loom," I murmured, pointing with my thumb to the back office.

"My name is Daniel," he said, hand extended. "I'm staying in this hotel."

"Aha." I nodded as I shook his hand. It was warm and soft yet firm.

I felt like an idiot. I wanted to tell him my name but all that came out was an "aha." It made me sad, not only because of my stupidity, but I also came to think of *Jayeechi*—the songs of love.

"And your name is?" he asked, pulling me out of the abyss into which I was falling.

"Yonna," I heard myself saying.

"Thanks, Yonna."

He took the gift and disappeared from the shop, while my heart tried jumping out of my mouth.

Chapter 24

THEA

"LIEBE, YOUR MOTHER MUST be very proud of you. Those are many presents," Thea told the young man wryly, noting that he often came to the shop to buy. He first bought a carpet, then a bag, and finally, a couple of Guajira blankets, if memory served her well. However, she discovered that he was not interested in the goods; she often caught him glancing over her shoulder toward the office and the loom.

"Yes, I think she's proud of me. She asked me to buy all the local crafts I could," he remarked absently.

"Anything else?" Thea asked, holding back laughter, amused at the hunt he had mounted on Yonna.

"No, no ... May I ask you: Are you from Austria?"

"Germany, why?"

"Well, you said *liebe* ..."

"Ahh. I'm sure you know how hard it is to forget your mother tongue. Where are you from?"

"Danish."

Thea didn't ask him anything else; it seemed apparent he didn't want to talk about himself. He paid and left the shop with hurried steps.

Thea went into the room where Yonna worked, only to find her pacing back and forth while rubbing her hands.

"Child, why did you not come out?"

With astonishment, Yonna asked, "Me? I have nothing to do out there." She turned back to the piece she was weaving.

Thea was sure Yonna liked the man and his attentions but was too shy and awkward to respond to him. The old woman could sense it—after twelve years of living in the same house with Yonna, she could not be deceived. Yonna didn't want him to hear her stammer, as she often did when nervous.

This man has swept Yonna off her feet, she thought.

Yonna, who never complained, now mentioned feelings of something cold in her stomach. She lost her appetite and had to stay in bed with fever, sweating, and weeping. Now Thea knew the reason why and she would have wished that Yonna herself told her everything, but the young girl was not giving anything away, so she asked the *Zapuanas* instead.

From them, Thea learned that the young man, Daniel, never took his eyes off Yonna. They had seen him hanging around the store, no longer interested in the goods, but simply waiting for the opportunity to see Yonna for even a second.

Yonna thought that Thea would scare the *alijuuna* away but it was exactly the opposite. Thea thought it was charming, seeing him so sad when he left the shop, unable to catch a glimpse of Yonna.

"*Liebe*, do you like that man?"

"Yes," she murmured, opening her eyes in amazement at her own answer.

"Child, if you like him, you have to leave the back office. Do you understand?"

"I get nervous and drop things," she replied while watching her hands.

They heard a voice from the doorway. "May I interrupt? Actually, I came because of you."

Yonna and Thea turned toward the door and there was the *alijuuna* holding the bag Thea sold him only minutes ago.

Yonna stood behind the old woman, using her as a shield.

"Ma'am, would you allow me to go on a date with her?"

Thea ushered him to the front of the shop and closed the door on their way out.

"It is not my decision but I do care for her and I am responsible for her." Thea stopped her explanation when she noticed the *Zapuanas* peeking out from the shop, whispering and giggling. "The show is over," she announced with fake solemnity.

Once they were out of sight, Thea turned her attention back to the man. "And you, what do you want with Yonna?" Thea braced herself for his answer, keeping in mind the feelings Yonna had expressed for him.

"I like her a lot," he confessed, holding Thea's gaze. The sincerity in his eyes disarmed her. "I know that Yonna lives with you and that she isn't seeing someone else. My gut also tells me she likes me, too. I'm willing to wait however long I need to, but I kindly ask for your blessing and for you not to stand in the way. If Yonna wants me, I won't let anything in this world stand between us."

"*Liebe* Daniel, I am so delighted that those are your intentions because if you hurt her, there will be nothing in this world standing between me and breaking your balls. Are we clear?"

The young man burst out laughing but Thea noticed he was shaking.

"Something else," she warned, "Yonna is not the kind of woman you take to the movies."

"Are you going to help me?"

"Of course, but not because of you."

"What can I do to make her go out with me?" he asked, peeking over her shoulder toward the office, hoping to see Yonna.

"Earn her trust, but first you have to tell me your story."

"Everything?" he asked, raising his eyebrows.

"Do you have a problem with that?"

DANIEL

"DURING THE FALL of 1943, in a small town in southern Sweden, the *luthier* Ari Kreutzer sought refuge from the Gestapo. It was a journey of only three miles, which he made, camouflaged in a fisherman's boat. By entering Sweden, Ari obtained his residence permit, just as many other Jews in the same situation."

"A *luthier*? Did your granddad make fiddles?" Thea asked skeptically.

"Yes and he was the only one in my family who made instruments," he replied before continuing, "Ari met Ruth, and when the German occupation forces left Denmark, both returned to Copenhagen and married. They were my grandparents."

"What about your parents?" Thea inquired.

"Ari and Ruth had two sons: my father Daniel, whom I was named after, and my uncle Aaron. My father married my mother, Anne-Marie. A few years after I was born, Aaron disappeared without a trace. I don't know the details since I was so young when it happened ..."

"Where are your parents now?"

"They live in Denmark."

"Any brothers or sisters?"

"Only a sister; her name is Ruth, named after our grandmother."

"What about you?"

"I'm an engineer. I work as a consultant in the Operations Management Department in El Tablazo; I've been working there for the last three years."

"You're a little far from El Tablazo, don't you think?"

"It's less than an hour by plane."

"You speak very good Spanish ..."

"I took Spanish lessons prior to coming here and continued when I was settled."

An uncomfortable feeling was growing in his stomach. He didn't appreciate the way this woman wondered, almost seeming to doubt his intentions.

"Are you on vacation? You spend quite a lot of time here in Maracaibo ..." Thea remarked with a touch of sarcasm, fully unnecessary, as far as Daniel was concerned.

It's obvious that if I want to get to know Yonna, I have to hang around the shop, he thought. He was even tempted to say it but knew that it would only have made matters worse. He opted for diplomacy.

"There's a minor issue with my contract. I sent it back, suggesting some corrections, but the papers didn't make it on time to the legal department, so the old contract expired and I was dumped out of the system. They are working on it. In fact, this is the second time it has happened."

"Are you married?" Thea asked, her pale blue eyes piercing Daniel.

"Jesus, no," he replied, exasperated. "May I have some water?"

"Yes, of course. Sorry for my manners."

Thea called one of the *Zapuanas* and asked her for some water. The girl walked away nodding and returned minutes later with a jug and two glasses. She put everything on the counter to the right of the cash register and disappeared into the back room.

"Why aren't you married?"

"I guess I haven't met the right woman."

The two *Zapuanas* came back and announced that they had finished their work for the day. Thea beckoned him to wait a moment while she walked them to the exit. When they left, a tourist came into the shop, asking if they knew of an open pharmacy nearby. While Daniel stood there waiting, he wondered why Yonna almost never left the workroom.

"But you've had other girlfriends?" Thea asked, resuming the interrogation.

That's none of your business, he thought.

"Yes, I guess we were too young. Besides, it never ended up in something more concrete," he replied, forcing a smile.

"What makes you think that Yonna is the right woman?"

"I don't know if she is but I want to find out. All I can see in Yonna is modesty and detachment. Besides, she is very talented. I've never seen crafts like this," he said, holding the bag he bought high up in the air.

"How?"

"W-what do you mean how?" Daniel asked hesitantly.

"You say that Yonna radiates modesty and detachment."

"Well, she often goes barefoot, no jewelry, always with the Guajira robe," he ventured. "Maybe it's because she doesn't try hard; she's unassuming. She is so incredibly beautiful without realizing it."

Suddenly, Yonna came out. "Sorry," she muttered.

"It's okay," said Thea, encouraging her to come closer.

Daniel felt ice in his stomach and took a deep breath, holding it for a few seconds. He wanted to catch her eye but she again addressed Thea. "I was just wondering when we're going home."

He had the opportunity to appreciate the contrast of her copper eyes against the black hair that fell below her shoulders.

"It's my fault for keeping you," he hurried to say.

"Why don't you join us for dinner?" Thea proposed. Daniel was truly surprised. Judging by the interview, he thought it would be the last time he set foot in the shop.

"I would hate to trouble you like that," he lied.

"It would be a pleasure," said Yonna, smiling at him.

Now Daniel felt butterflies fluttering madly in his bowels. He accepted the invitation and begged heaven that Thea wouldn't think of preparing sauerkraut. The popular German dish, with its bitter, acidic cabbage, was more than enough to fill him with dread.

They agreed that Daniel would meet them at their place in two hours. He didn't want to show up empty-handed so he went back to his room, took a quick shower, and tried to find a florist. He walked a couple of blocks without much luck. Then just when he was about to give up, he spotted a hidden flower shop behind a newsstand.

A woman motioned that they were about to close, but Daniel guessed she saw the desperation painted on his face and decided to help.

Daniel ordered a bouquet of red and white roses, and she suggested adding some purple verbena flowers. He thought it was a little overkill since the flowers piled up like a bunch of grapes, but the woman grabbed a few strands of white verbena instead as she explained. She tied the whole thing in a bouquet packed in cellophane and wrapped it with curled gift ribbons.

He was glad he didn't protest since the results exceeded his expectations. He gave her a well-deserved tip and hurried out to have dinner with Yonna and Thea.

Chapter

26

DANIEL

HE KNOCKED ON their door and stepped back to observe the houses better. All of them were colorful, like the blue church at the end of the road. He inspected the flowers and ran his hand down his chest, as if to smooth his immaculately pressed shirt. Although he was happy with his appearance, his heart was beating fiercely.

It would be nice to have a cold Carlsberg, he thought.

A smiling Yonna opened the door and he instantly felt the urge to kiss her. A picture flashed in his mind of her as his wife, welcoming him home after a long day at work.

"Good evening," he heard himself saying, trying to push the words past the sand in his throat.

"Welcome, sir," she said, stepping aside to let him in.

Daniel handed her the flowers. She studied them and glanced back at him before her lips parted in a shy smile.

"*Jeyutse*, verbena flowers," she explained. "Sir, among my people, verbena is considered a sacred plant. Did you know that?"

He felt his knees weaken. *Get a grip!* He admonished himself.

"No," he admitted, "but I'm glad you like them. What is it that makes them sacred?"

"We use them to cure diseases. Sir, come in, please."

"I'll come in on one condition: stop being so formal," Daniel teased her.

"Okay, I'll do my best," she said, returning the smile and lowering her head.

She led him down a corridor. When they were halfway through, Thea came out to greet him.

"Daniel, welcome."

Yonna showed her the flowers and when she disappeared to find a vase for them, Thea gave him a thumbs up. The warm welcome seemed strange, compared to the hard questioning to which she subjected him only hours earlier.

"Well done, young man," she whispered.

They took him to the kitchen, reminiscent of the rustic German kitchens, with wood panels on the walls and the metal kitchen counter standing in the center.

Expensive taste, he thought, as he enjoyed the smell of *paella.*

"Have you ever eaten Wayuu dishes?" Thea asked him.

"No, but I'm open to whatever you have to offer."

"We're sure you'll like it. Don't you think so, Yonna?" asked Thea, attempting to engage her in the conversation.

She was busy arranging the flowers in the vase but managed to reply with a "yes."

Yonna was wearing a white Guajira tunica that accented the natural bronze color of her skin. Her thick mass of black hair was tied in a braid.

"Can I help?" he asked, trying to chill his thoughts.

"*Liebe* Yonna, I think Daniel can help you set the table, don't you think?"

"Yes, sure," she said, blushing slightly. Yonna left the room and returned a few minutes later, holding a folded white tablecloth. "Come, let's set the table."

He followed her silently down the hall and entered the dining room. The threshold was made of a varnished log. A massive mahogany table with eight seats stood in the center over a brown, rustic rug that did not seem Wayuu. The walls were white.

Yonna and Daniel spread the tablecloth. She went to a cupboard that displayed a collection of crystal glasses and crockery, where she retrieved the dishes. She explained how he should arrange the plates, as she opened a drawer from the same cupboard for the silverware, which she also handed him. After some brief instructions, she let him finish on his own.

Yonna disappeared down the hall and came back quickly with the flowers he had given her. She put the vase on the center of the table, stepping back to see it, and approved of the setting with a smile.

"We forgot the glasses," she exclaimed, clutching her head in an exaggerated shock.

When she lifted her arms, he could not help but admire the delicious curve of her breasts. Daniel averted his gaze as quickly as he could, afraid that Yonna would catch him red-handed. Fortunately, Yonna didn't seem to notice. She took the glasses they needed and placed them on the table.

Thea joined them, carrying a lavish tray of lobsters resting on a bed of lettuce leaves and tomato slices. Yonna hastened to move the flowers to give the tray plenty of room in the center.

"Wow," he said, admiring the impressive dinner they had prepared on such short notice. The sight of the meal reminded him that he hadn't eaten since breakfast.

Thea smiled and returned to the kitchen.

"What do you think?" Yonna wanted to know.

"I'm sure I'm going to like it."

Thea came back with two bowls. "Have you ever had *tostones*?" she asked.

"Yes, with fried fish."

"And *warepo* rice?" Yonna asked.

"I haven't but I want to give it a try," he assured her.

"Okay, take your seats," Yonna commanded as she removed the apron from Thea before going back to the kitchen. She returned with a bottle of white wine, which she handed to Daniel, along with a corkscrew.

They made him sit at the head of the table. The *warepo* rice was tasty, like *paella*, but the only thing in it was tiny shells. Yonna explained that this was the rice of the poor. The fishermen used *warepos* as bait.

They ate and laughed. Thea made him repeat the story of his life and he noticed that Yonna listened with genuine interest. He enjoyed seeing this beautiful Wayuu woman drinking white wine and enjoying herself in his company. Daniel laughed at himself for thinking that he was going to conquer her, when it was he who ended up falling at her feet.

Daniel had a hunch that he was sitting to the right of the woman he wanted to make his wife. He would have given his life to stay the whole night with them. He thanked God that a woman like Thea took such good care of Yonna, as it was obvious that Yonna had learned a myriad things under Thea's wings, things that she otherwise would never have had the opportunity to experience.

It was almost ten o'clock when he decided to go back to the hotel. He thanked them for the meal and Yonna walked him to the door.

"Thank you," was all she said as she hugged him. He felt her tiny body throbbing in his arms. It was instant, like a flash, but he didn't want to scare her so he left without kissing her.

Chapter 27

DANIEL

TIME PASSED with no news of Daniel's contract. He didn't worry since it wasn't the first time he had dealt with the same situation. In fact, he found it very convenient since Yonna's company was way more desirable than being on his own in the boring apartment at the Petrochemical complex.

They dined together almost every evening, except for rare occasions when he declined the invitation, as he didn't want to become a nuisance.

Gradually, he managed to get Yonna out of the shop for strolls around the hotel, but the progress they had made plummeted one rainy afternoon. They were on their way back to the shop when a wave of tourists left their bus and ran into the hotel like a herd of buffalo to avoid the rain.

The people made her panic and she took refuge against his chest. He almost had to drag her back to the shop. When the mass of tourists scattered through the lobby, Yonna ran straight to the shop and locked herself in the office. Thea, who was standing near the cash register, gave him a mean stare, assuming that Yonna's reaction was his fault. He explained to her what happened.

"I need to know what's going on to understand her phobia," he announced, unable to repress his frustration.

"*Liebe* Daniel, she is the one who should tell you," Thea replied in despair, tears clouding her eyes. "All I can say is that you have achieved something no one else has: you have helped her leave that room. It worries me because I don't know what will happen to her the day I die ..."

"Please don't say that," he managed to say, "I just hope she tells me soon what's going on."

There was a pause, and Yonna didn't emerge from the workroom.

"I better go," he said, on his way to the exit.

"Promise you will come tomorrow," Thea pleaded from the counter.

"Sure I will," he assured her with a touch of concern.

Daniel left the shop with a sense of uncertainty that knocked his spirits. He went to the lobby to pick up the room key and the receptionist handed him a note.

It was a message from the Petrochemical complex; it seemed that the issue with his contract was resolved and he had to return as soon as possible. He should have been happy about the news but he was far from it.

He ran to the shop and told Thea that he had fly to El Tablazo on the first flight he could squeeze into, but he was coming back Friday evening.

"Go in and tell her," Thea encouraged.

"Sure she wants to talk to me?"

"*Liebe*, I don't know. Why don't you try?"

The *Zapuanas* were leaning on the door of the back shop, whispering, but they disappeared when they saw Daniel approach the workroom. He knocked gently and opened the door without waiting for Yonna's response.

When he entered, he found Yonna sitting on the bench in front of a half-woven mat. Her eyes were bloodshot and her nose glowed red, like she had been frantically rubbing it with the crumpled paper towel in her hand.

He approached and stroked the outline of her jaw.

"Sorry if I scared you," Daniel managed to say.

She lowered her head. "You haven't," she whispered, looking down.

"I'm glad to hear that," he said, taking her hand in his. "See, I just got a message from my employer. I have to fly to El Tablazo as soon as possible."

112

When she heard the news, she met his eyes. Daniel thought for a moment she wanted to say something, but she pursed her lips and lowered her head.

"I'll be back here Friday evening."

"I wouldn't blame you if you didn't want to come back," she murmured, staring at her hands.

"Yonna, I'll return on Friday, okay?" Daniel gently turned her jaw so they could face each other.

With their faces so close, almost touching, he grazed her lips with his. She smiled and for the first time ever, she ran her fingers along his jaw. He would have given anything to prolong this moment, but the reality of the impending trip broke the magic.

"I have to pack but I'll see you on Friday." He stood up slowly and headed toward the door.

"Have a good trip." At that distance, she seemed helpless, tiny.

"Yonna, I'll be back on Friday and then … we can talk," he said, holding the doorknob.

Yonna jumped up and ran toward him. She closed her arms around his neck and buried her face on his chest. "Please come back," she begged in a low voice.

In other circumstances, that hug would have awakened the flame he had been extinguishing with cold showers all this time, but the impact of her reaction to the tourists turned off his system. Daniel hugged her for a while and they left the workroom hand in hand. Thea smiled on their way to the exit, where Yonna and Daniel parted with a brief touch on the lips.

Chapter

28

DANIEL

WHEN DANIEL ARRIVED in El Tablazo, it was as if time stood still; Yonna was all he thought of. He could have snuck into one of the offices to call her, but he had been away from work for so long that it did not seem wise.

Later that day, he found out that the upper management summoned him not to renew the contract but to terminate it. The petrochemical company decided to close two mega projects: one in the liquefied gas department and the other in the olefins camp, where he worked. The bosses' strategy resulted in the dismissal of seventeen international consultants.

The managers held a go-home meeting to inform them about the decision, where they were asked to hand over identification cards, keys, and any other materials the management considered vital to the operations. Daniel felt like a criminal, since they weren't allowed to talk to their respective supervisors. The managers also made a point about the confidentiality agreement they all had signed upon starting in the company. The company gave them six months' salary and promised to contact them, in case the situation changed. They walked out of the premises with an escort to make sure they didn't remove sensitive information from the plant. The worst part, though, was that they were not allowed to say goodbye to their colleagues.

Now that nothing was holding Daniel in El Tablazo, he went to the apartment to collect his things and fly back to Maracaibo. He went straight to the bedroom and noticed that someone had messed up his stuff in the suitcase he had left on the bed. Although it was disturbed, nothing seemed missing. Even stranger, everything was clean. No traces of dust on any surface that Daniel ran his fingers across.

Daniel opened the drawers of the dresser to take his belongings: socks, underwear, CDs. He checked under the bed and pulled out a pair of running shoes and a bunch of old issues of the *American Chemical Society Journal*. He stacked them all and placed them on the dresser to be disposed of by the housekeeper. In the nightstand drawer, he found an old copy of a Malcolm Gladwell book he never finished, and laughed at the irony of his job situation when he picked *The Five Dysfunctions of a Team*. He went through the closet but there was not much—just a couple of jackets covered with plastic bags.

Daniel went to the bathroom and the bulb blew out when he tried to turn on the light. *No longer my problem*, he thought. When he opened the cabinet, there were only aftershave lotion, a couple of Gillette disposable razors, and a brand new roll-on deodorant.

He secured his suitcases and left the room. When he was about to close the door for the last time, something on the wall caught his attention and he realized he almost left something important. Two posters, bought and framed by Ruth and Mom back in Denmark, announced Muddy Waters concerts in The Checkerboard Lounge and Voters Club. Daniel went back to fetch them. He closed all the doors and left the key in the mailbox at the reception area, with a note giving his landlord notice.

Daniel took a taxi to Cabimas Airport and found out there were no available seats to Maracaibo. Since he was not willing to wait two days to fly and with no place to live, he decided to drive a rented car for the eleven hours that separated him from Yonna.

Chapter

29

DANIEL

THE ONLY ADVANTAGE of driving at night on Zulian roads was that the air chilled. It was obviously a dark, dusty, and dangerous road, so Daniel was grateful to have something keeping him awake. Fortunately, the car he rented didn't break down.

When he was too tired to continue, he checked in a family hotel near Santa Barbara, threw himself on the bed, too exhausted to undress, and fell asleep within minutes. The next day, a knock on the door woke him. The owner was worried because it was already after noon and he had not yet left the room.

His body felt like lead. Daniel took a long shower and went to the dining room, hoping for something to eat before hitting the road. They had leftovers from breakfast, but the orange islands of fat, floating on the surface of what they offered as bologna pasta sauce, took away his hunger. He was still stuck with paying for an extra day because according to their rules, checkout was at 9:30 a.m.

Daniel filled the gas tank at the first station he saw and drove to Maracaibo without stopping.

When he returned to the hotel, he left the bags and all he had brought from his apartment in El Tablazo and went down to the lobby. He glanced at the craft shop, hoping to see Yonna. Although the lights were on, the "closed" sign hung on the window of the store.

They went home and forgot to turn the lights off, he thought.

Daniel was about to go upstairs when Yonna came out of the workroom. He knocked on the glass door and she ran to open it when she saw him. Yonna let him in and threw her arms around him without a word.

"I thought you weren't coming," she said at last, her hands pressed against his chest.

"I promised I would," he replied with a smile.

"Do you want to come over for dinner?"

"Love to. Where's Thea?" he asked, wondering why he didn't hear her moving around the shop.

"She's away in Caracas, buying stuff for the shop. She'll be back tomorrow."

"Have you been alone all day?" Daniel asked without hiding his astonishment.

"Not at all, the *Zapuanas* were here, too."

"Are you sure it's okay to have dinner at your place?"

"Yes."

They took a taxi. It was so nice to have her by his side again. Her presence filled him with energy, like anything was possible. All traces of the long journey were gone and no one would have guessed that only a couple of days before, he had been fired and his future in Maracaibo was uncertain.

There was no need to worry Yonna with his problems, though. Daniel still had hope of finding a job with another oil company, since people with his profile weren't easy to find.

They ended up eating slices of bread, blue cheese, grapes, tangerines, and bits of chopped onions. They devoured the whole shebang on the kitchen counter. Yonna took a bottle of white wine from the fridge and two glasses.

They did not say much; instead, they exchanged glances, laughed, and ate. Suddenly, Yonna disappeared. At first, he thought she was in her bedroom. He called her but she did not reply, so Daniel poked his head in her room. She was not there, so he kept searching for her in other rooms until he found her standing beside the bathtub.

His heart began to pound.

"Yonna?"

"Come."

Daniel took a deep breath and walked slowly, afraid of misjudging the scene in front of him.

Yonna leaned on his arm and immersed herself in the tub with her clothes on. Tiny white verbena petals and tangerine segments spread across the steamy water. When she dipped in, they moved to the rhythm of a gentle wave. She never took her eyes off him.

The vision of Yonna in the bath was similar to that of a virgin. The Guajira dress was soaked up above her chest and made her curves more suggestive than if she had been submerged completely naked.

He was speechless and felt the slight tremor of his lips. She beckoned him to enter the bathtub and he did the only thing he could think of— took the wallet out of his back pocket and joined her, fully dressed.

That broke the ice and they both laughed at their soaked clothes, Yonna in her Guajira tunica and Daniel in his grey pants and light blue shirt. They sat there, facing each other. Yonna took his hand to soothe his nerves, when it seemed that it should be him comforting her. She took a tangerine section and slowly touched his lips with it.

She told him about her mother, her granny *piache*, and how she learned to knit when she was only a little girl. Yonna narrated about her brothers, her Wayuu life, the *chicha maya* fest, and the subsequent slaughter where her entire family perished. She described the horrors she lived at the hands of the police, the vomiting fits, and how she spent whole nights listening to the voice of her *piache*. Yonna told Daniel how the policemen left her on the road to Paraguaipoa, the harsh existence with *la señora* Meche, the constant threat of Tomás, and how Thea became her angel.

At times, his hands clenched in anger and powerlessness for hearing so much misery. She wept quietly, almost whispering, and Daniel wept with her.

"It's over, Yonna," he managed to say, as he took her hand.

"My *piache* said so," Yonna muttered between sobs.

They stayed in silence until Yonna rose from the tub, her wet clothes adhering to her body like a sheer second skin. She took her soaked tunica off and dropped it on the floor. On her way out of the bathroom, she turned and glanced at Daniel.

"Please be gentle," he heard her say, and with a slight nod she disappeared down the hall.

Daniel left the tub, took his clothes off, and followed her.

Chapter

30

"YONNA, WILL YOU marry me?" Daniel asked me between kisses.

"Yes."

I realized that I belonged to the *alijuuna* the first time he stepped into the shop, when the urge to weep assailed me, as I was convinced that a man like him was already taken. In my dreams, I asked my *piache* about Daniel and she approved of him.

"Daniel won my heart," Thea would say to the old ladies who frequented the store, "because he was the only one who made her go to places other than to the shop and back home again."

She was right; if Daniel had not come into the shop that day, I'm sure I could have stayed *yüütüwaa*, a lonely Wayuu.

I wistfully realized that I wouldn't marry another Wayuu like me because of what happened to my family, and after moving to Thea's home, I no longer lived like a Wayuu. What I kept from my culture were my rugs and the Guajira tunica I always wore. The only thing I knew about my name was that everyone called me Yonna, my granny was my *piache* like my mom, and my dad was Noshua. Among my people, you didn't need to know more.

That was why, after buying my freedom in the stall of *la señora* Meche, Thea had brought me to the civil registry to establish my identity—she needed to know more.

There were no birth records among the Wayuu people, and the name of each person was associated with the function we came to carry out within our caste. When the woman at the registry asked me how old I was, I had no idea. After eyeing me up and down, she decided that I must have been about fourteen. Even though I wasn't completely sure, I also thought that I must have been around the age she suggested, so I didn't contradict her.

The woman filled out a form and announced that since I did not know my own birthdate, she deducted fourteen years from the current date and wrote it down. She took my right thumb, soaked it in ink, and pressed it on a card.

"As we don't know Yonna's family name, why don't we use mine?" Thea suggested, fearing that the woman could also take a random surname for me. She nodded as she wrote and asked Thea to spell her surname. She called an assistant to take my picture.

The man made me stand against a white wall and flashed a neon white light at me with his black machine. The device spat out a paper with four copies of my photo. He shook it a few times, as if it were wet, and handed it to the woman who kept writing notes in a musty book. Soon, she handed me a laminated card that read:

Republic of Venezuela
Identity Card
Yonna Weiss
Born May 17, 1983

Twelve years ago, Thea gave me her name, and I'll always be grateful. Twelve years ago, I kept the identity card in my nightstand drawer, since I never had to use it. Only when I realized I was about to be married did I have the poignant revelation that I had become *shiatapünaa* Wayuu, that is to say, half Wayuu and half *alijuuna*.

"Are you sad?" Thea asked me, and I spotted a hint of concern in her eyes.

"Not at all," I answered, but I knew that it didn't convince her.

"Daniel is a good man, Yonna. He really loves you," she said, patting my hand.

"I don't want to leave you alone here in Maracaibo," I muttered, fighting back the tears.

"*Liebe*, that's nonsense," Thea assured me. "You can visit me as much as you want."

I had dared more and more to push myself outside on my own since Daniel walked into my life, and the best days I'd ever had were when I was with him. Yet as the wedding preparations got closer to the day, the idea of leaving Thea and the *Zapuanas* was becoming unbearable. They too were part of my family.

Chapter

31

DANIEL

WHILE DANIEL WAS SETTING the table, a wave of concern began to build up in his stomach. He tried not to think of it while arranging flowers the way Yonna had taught him. The final result wasn't satisfactory but he sucked at arranging flowers anyway. "Flowers are not my thing," he admitted.

Daniel had asked Thea and Yonna to wait at the store a little longer than usual; he wanted to surprise them with homemade dinner. Not only did he plan this as a celebration of the wedding, which was only a few days away, but he also needed a way to gently break the news of his unemployment.

The original idea had been to take them out to DaVinci's for dinner and let them know then. However, the evening started on the wrong foot when Yonna unknowingly ordered carpaccio, a raw meat dish. Since she hated raw meat, he traded it with his mozzarella in *carozza*. By the end of the evening, when Daniel thought he had gathered enough courage, Yonna and Thea began talking about the possibility of opening a craft shop in El Tablazo. There was so much enthusiasm in their voices that he did not dare break the spell.

Daniel was running out of time so he promised himself to announce the news during dinner. No more excuses.

The smell of stuffed rump steak in the oven hung throughout the house, and the fried bananas lay ready on a plate. He decided to give the dish an international flavor by making it the way they did in Denmark—with cream, butter, and a pinch of pepper, with mashed potatoes on the side instead of rice. He got the stuffed rump steak recipe from Thea, who had served it a few months before.

The uneasiness was settling in his stomach and he would have given anything for a cold Carlsberg, although a glass of wine would do, too. This reminded him to open the bottle of Chilean Pinot Noir 2006 (which he had found in a little import store downtown) to let it breathe.

When Daniel grabbed the neck of the bottle, he noticed that his hands were soaked in sweat. He wiped them on his pants and tried to open the bottle. He sank and turned the tip of the corkscrew and pulled the plug in one try, as he heard noises by the front door.

Must be them, he thought.

When Daniel poked his head from the kitchen, he saw an exhausted Thea. Behind her was Yonna, holding some bags. Thea gave him a weak smile and Yonna threw her arms around him.

"Get a room," Thea joked.

They wanted to help him carry the trays of food to the table, but Daniel insisted that it was his treat. It made him sad to see the joy and anticipation in their faces, especially because he had arranged the whole thing to break bad news.

They sat down and the women took turns telling him the details of their shopping tour.

"Daniel?" Yonna called his attention. "What is it? Why don't you say much?"

"I have something to tell you," he stammered.

Given his sad expression, Yonna sensed the clouds in the landscape but did not utter a word. She held her breath and waited for the storm.

"*Verdammt!* You're married, aren't you?" Thea exploded.

"No, no," he replied, horrified by what Yonna might think but also surprised by Thea's reaction. Aside from the day she questioned his intentions for Yonna, she had only shown exquisite manners. He had never heard her curse before, let alone in German.

"It's not that," he assured them.

126

"What happened, then?" Yonna asked, remaining calm.

Now or never, he thought. Daniel filled his lungs with air.

"I lost my job in El Tablazo. I have three months' salary left, but without a job, I will have to leave the country."

A mantle of silence fell heavily upon them.

"There must be something wrong, Daniel. After so many years, they only gave you three months?" Thea remarked, breaking the stillness.

"My contract expired three months ago," he whispered, avoiding their eyes.

"What?" they asked in shocked unison.

"But you've been traveling all this time," Yonna added.

"Yes, that's true. I've been traveling to find a job in another company, but there's nothing."

"What do you have in mind?" Yonna asked, afraid to hear the answer.

"There's not much to do unless I work. Otherwise, I can stay here for the next three months, but when my permit expires, I will have to leave the country."

"Even if you marry Yonna?"

"I haven't figured that out, Thea, but one thing is sure: I need a job ..." Daniel paused to let them digest the news.

Yonna played with her fork and Thea drank the rest of her wine in one gulp.

"I didn't think it was fair to marry you without telling you about this," he ventured to say.

"I really appreciate it," Yonna said. Daniel seemed to catch a hint of sarcasm in her words. He did not know if her flushed cheeks were the product of the wine or because she was fuming.

"This is something you need to discuss in private," Thea said, standing up slowly. "If I may, I'll leave you both alone," she added as she disappeared down the hall with tired steps.

"Why didn't you tell us?" Yonna asked once Thea had left.

"I thought I could get a job elsewhere; I didn't want to worry you, but now that I'm running out of time and every single door I knock on is closed ... I can't keep hiding this, Yonna. You understand what this means?"

"Yeah, I think you're trying to say you're flying back to your country, aren't you?" A couple of teardrops rolled down her beautiful face.

"I still want to marry you, Yonna," he said, wiping away her tears. "I want to take you with me to Denmark."

"I thought we were moving to El Tablazo. That was hard enough, but living in Denmark? I can't leave Thea alone," Yonna replied.

"Don't even think about it, young woman," cried Thea from the hallway. They jumped as she broke into the dining room. "If I left everything in Germany to follow Gualtiero, why can't you do the same for Daniel?"

Chapter

32

WE COULDN'T MAKE Thea change her mind about coming with us to Denmark; neither would she let me stay with her.

"As newlyweds, you should spend time on your own," she insisted.

I hadn't been outside Maracaibo for a very long time, so the idea of a trip to Denmark provided the opportunity to start a new chapter in my life. I was torn between two contradictory feelings; it was really sad to leave Thea, but at the same time, I was thrilled to start this 'couple's journey' with Daniel.

Daniel and I were married at the registry office. The only witnesses were Thea and the *Zapuanas*. We put off the honeymoon so I could spend as much time with Thea as possible. After the wedding, time flew like a flock of flamingos over a lagoon. We shopped for days, as Thea insisted that I had to dress in the European fashion, and Daniel suggested that a crash course in English for me wouldn't be a bad idea. Thea tried to find out some courses in Danish too, but that language was so exotic that no one taught it in Venezuela.

I reluctantly accepted, but although it took time away from Thea, I must admit that the little bit of English I learned before we left helped me manage at the international airports.

Thanks to *Mareygua*, I wasn't traveling alone. For someone who had never been abroad, it was a tremendous cultural shock, but Daniel was right there with me and patiently explained what to do in each new situation.

"A new world is about to open for you," Thea said with wet eyes at the

Chinita airport when we were about to board the plane. I held her tight to imprint her smell of lemongrass in my subconscious and thanked her for all that she had done for me. I hoped she knew she had a holy status in my heart.

With a promise between Thea and me to call each other as often as we could, I left Maracaibo. It struck me that Thea aged in a matter of days. Her pale blue eyes had a yellowish edge, her skin was parchment-like, and her gait became slower. There was not much left of the thick silver hair she boasted in her best days; the energy she radiated was gone, too.

The whole trip took thirty-two hours and had two stopovers, one at Simon Bolivar Airport and the second in Frankfurt. Once there, Daniel told me we were in Thea's country.

I would never forget my experience in the restrooms at the airport in Frankfurt. I sat down to pee and when I stood, it flushed without my touching anything. My *piache* would have died of laughter if she had seen me, I'm sure.

"It has an infrared sensor which detects when the person walks away," Daniel explained.

"I hope this thing didn't snap pictures of my butt," I said jokingly.

When we finally passed customs at the Copenhagen airport, Daniel's mom was there, waiting for us on the other side of the exit door.

"No need to be worried, Yonna," Daniel assured me, seconds before we walked through the door. "I've told her so many good things that she's been counting the days to meet you."

Anne-Marie reminded me of Thea in the old days, when she dragged me out of *la señora* Meche's stall. Her silver hair was long enough to cover her ears and she boasted the same hazel eyes as Daniel's. She had a very slender figure, dressed in delicate lace up to her neck. A thick gold bracelet hung from one arm; a black-strapped watch sat on the other. Her wedding ring glinted in the sunlight, drawing attention to the bouquet she carried.

Without saying much, she gave me a hug, and I realized that Anne-Marie was as tall as Daniel. I thought I was going to disappear in her arms. I pulled back a little bit to have a better look at her; with moist eyes, she handed me the flowers. It was a lovely bouquet of tiny white and pale green blossoms.

Her gesture touched me so much that I hugged her again. This time, my cheek rested on her chest by accident, which made me blush with embarrassment. We all laughed and it proved to be a good icebreaker.

"Please tell her that I truly appreciate her welcome," I told Daniel. He was going to have to be the translator for a while. With a smile, he relayed what I said and she gave me another hug.

At first, Anne-Marie tried to speak in English, but my English was so poor that I asked them to switch to Danish, so I could observe the city and they could catch up with each other.

It was a long trip. The stress of the flight and leaving Thea had drained all my energy like water running down a gutter. I remembered walking into an underground parking garage where hundreds of cars were parked neatly within boundary lines painted on the ground. I was impressed that the structure wasn't full of trash.

We drove away in a fancy black car that smelled new; Daniel sat at the wheel. I insisted on taking the back seat so they could talk as I enjoyed the view. As we left the airport, our parking ticket was swallowed by a machine. The toll bar rose as if by magic and we drove away. I had seen some of those in Maracaibo, but it had booths where a guard took the ticket and received the payment.

It was getting darker and the city was deserted. I saw no mountains, no speeding cars, no one running red lights, and—best of all—no drivers honking their horns. There was no noise, no smog, no stalls. I would have loved to have had Thea by my side. I sent her a greeting through my *piache*.

As I was thinking about the two most important women in my life, I caught my husband's eyes watching me through the rear view mirror. I blew him a kiss and he told me that his mom had found a nice house for us to live in. I thanked her once more, this time in Spanish, and she nodded, smiling.

Thanks to the lack of potholes and the wonderful suspension of the car, I fell asleep until we reached the house.

Chapter

33

(2010)

SPONTANEITY WAS THE essence of the Wayuu people. We were not afraid of praising the virtues of others or showing up uninvited for a short visit to a family member. To visit a relative here in Denmark, however, you had to make an appointment ahead of time, but it didn't take me too long to fully understand why it would be a good idea to call first. Still, I'd never figure out why you had to make an appointment for a haircut, even when there were no customers at the beauty parlor when you stepped in.

I admired that the Danes did not use bad weather as an excuse for not going to work. "There is no such thing as bad weather, only the wrong outfit," people would say. If it snowed, people would pull their sleds and dart after work to ride the hills with their kids.

Yet what I loved the most was that they didn't have the same notion of age as the locals had in Maracaibo. In Denmark, you were never too old to learn new skills, attend courses, or participate in a sporting event.

The Danes resembled the Wayuu people in that they valued the power of a spoken agreement. A handshake was enough to close a minor deal and in a majority of cases, people told the truth.

We moved into a beautiful home in the city of Farum.

"The house has been empty for quite a long time," said Anne-Marie when she handed us the keys. "There was an older couple interested but they gave up. As you know, Daniel, this is a quiet place and Ms.

133

Frederiksen takes care that everyone in the neighborhood is nice and civil."

Daniel smiled.

"Who's Ms. Frederiksen?" I asked Daniel.

"Some call her 'the Rottweiler'," said Daniel, who translated what Anne-Marie was saying. She lowered her voice, afraid that someone could hear as she continued, "Ms. Frederiksen is a retired nurse and she can be a little bit opinionated about people parking inconveniently and that kind of thing, but she is a very sweet person and a good friend of mine."

"A spinster?" Yonna ventured to ask.

"No, not at all." Anne-Marie explained, "She was married, her husband died abroad, and there's Peter, her son, but he lives in Copenhagen.

"As for the rest of the neighbors, don't worry. To the right, there's the Ravn family. Liva works from home and her husband works as an economist, I believe. They have a teen daughter; Tara, I think is her name. She is adopted from Africa."

"Mom, how do you know all that?" Daniel asked, clearly appalled at how much she knew about her neighbors.

"I know that the fact that I don't talk much with people is probably why we have such good relations with everyone here. Anyone can tell that lovely teen is adopted, though; her chocolate skin gives her away."

After catching me yawning a couple of times, Anne-Marie glanced at her watch and realized how late it was. "Well, I guess you must be exhausted from the long trip, so I'll leave you to rest. I'll stay in touch."

She waved as she headed to the main entrance. When she left, I couldn't hold back a question I had been wondering about. "Daniel, I wonder why your father wasn't here to welcome you. Is it because of me?"

"It's a long story, Yonna, but believe me when I tell you that it's not because of you; it's because of himself. Let's go to bed, okay?" Daniel answered with a weak smile.

Due to his unemployment, Daniel devoted as much time as he could to me. For the next few days, we stayed rolled up in bed until noon, made love in every corner of our home, and smeared our bodies with every edible sweet thing we found in the kitchen, cleaning it off with each other's kisses.

Reluctantly, Daniel and I did eventually go sightseeing. We went to see all of the city's attractions and hurried back home to make love until exhaustion closed our eyes.

Unfortunately for me, Daniel accepted the position of operations manager at an oil company headquartered in Lyngby. He would leave with the first light of day and return home in the dark.

Anne-Marie was also with me as much as she could when Daniel began working again. That sweet woman visited to make sure I was doing fine. When she learned that I wove rugs, not only did she fall in love with my work, she also provided me with the materials I needed to continue. I told her about Thea and how my *piache* whispered the patterns of the rugs to me.

My father-in-law, however, was a lying bastard who had an affair with another woman. I first met him by accident, when I showed up at their house unannounced. After ringing the bell a couple of times, I thought nobody was home. I was about to leave when I heard noises in the tool shed at the end of the garden.

I opened the door, expecting to find Anne-Marie working on her begonias. Instead, there he was with his pants rolled down to his ankles, leaning over someone on top of a chest freezer. His pale skin and bird-like legs gave him the appearance of a ghostly vision. After a second, I realized he was riding a woman similar to a geisha who seemed to be having a great time. The problem, aside from his marriage, of course, was that she could easily be his granddaughter.

He beckoned me to join them. I just slammed the door and ran out of the house.

We, the Wayuu people, accepted polygamy, and that was why I initially decided not to mention the incident to Daniel. Yet after much thought, I scrapped the idea. The clown was deceiving Anne-Marie and she needed to know. That was when I realized how impractical it was to be spontaneous.

Now more than ever, I wanted to learn Danish to understand what was going on around me, but I was forced to wait almost four months since that was what it took for the Immigration Service to process my visa application. Soon after I obtained the visa, I received a letter stating that I would be taking classes for foreigners to learn Danish.

It was hard work since I didn't have a good education, much less good study habits, but I was determined to speak my husband's language. When I mastered the basics, I borrowed books with matching cassettes from the library, so I could listen to the pronunciation of words while reading the text.

Anne-Marie often invited us to have lunch during the weekends, but after what I saw in my in-laws' garden, I preferred to avoid her husband.

"*Mi amor*," said Daniel, "I want you to be friends with Ruth." He insisted but I didn't share his enthusiasm. Ruth was sweet and patient with my linguistic shortcomings, but when we were alone, she did not have the same patience to explain things. She was sharp in her answers and on more than one occasion, openly mocked my ignorance.

The more I learned to speak Danish, the more I understood the context of what was happening within my new family, and the pieces slowly fell into place. At first, I attributed the coldness between Daniel and his dad to a cultural issue. They weren't rude to each other, but the way Daniel tensed his body when he was close to his father and how the old man frowned when talking to him convinced me that there was something under the surface.

I also suspected that Anne-Marie, who won my heart without much effort, was aware of her husband's escapades. They sat at the table next to each other but never exchanged glances. When the old man started to talk, Anne-Marie would leave the table under the pretext of fetching something in the kitchen. If Anne-Marie started the conversation, her husband would whisper things in Ruth's ear.

I never saw them holding hands or expressing mutual affection, just as I never saw them bickering. It was like an unspoken agreement. They tolerated each other in the presence of others solely in a vain attempt to keep up appearances.

Chapter
34

DANIEL
(2009)

"I'M A LUCKY man," he muttered while admiring Yonna in the mirror, watching as she moved around without noticing his stare. He just could not get enough of her.

Daniel froze the first time he saw her. He would never forget the red Guajira tunica she was wearing, her coal-black hair spilling over her shoulders, and her lips like an appetizing ripe fruit. He tried to catch her coppery eyes, though she did not notice.

He was convinced that he would never see her again. She had entered the craft shop at the hotel and he figured she must have come in to buy something and disappeared forever, but a few days later, Daniel was on his way out of the hotel when he saw her in the shop.

Now Daniel was almost sure she worked at the shop, so he decided to try his luck. He was glad he did. That decision landed him a wife with such a talent and resilience after all she'd been through, insanely beautiful, who was currently busy readying herself for Christmas Eve at his parents' place.

Yonna hadn't been sleeping well, though. She also complained of needing to pee more often. "I'm always chilled to the bones," she said.

He had also noticed she was tired a lot, regardless of what she did to conceal the light gray shadows under her eyes.

"Daniel, are you sure we don't have to wear something more formal?"

Yonna asked, pulling him back to the present.

"You're beautiful," he said with genuine admiration. She had a natural, simple beauty even after jumping out of bed in the morning.

"Yonna, the only stranger is Ruth's date," Daniel assured her.

No matter what he said, she tried on three different outfits until she reluctantly picked the black flannel dress—the first one she showed him. When they were ready, Daniel picked up two bottles of wine and the bags with the presents, and they walked past the six houses that separated them from his parents.

In other circumstances, he would have liked to live in another city, far away from Dad. He thought it would be good for Yonna having Mom around, though, and he guessed he was right. They seemed to have grown fond of each other.

When they arrived, Mom opened the door, wearing a huge smile and an apron over her white shirt and jeans. The whole house smelled of duck with pepper. Daniel closed his eyes and enjoyed the Christmas smell that he had so missed while in Maracaibo. All three of them hugged. Dad said something from the living room, but it was muffled with their voices.

"Haven't Ruth and her boyfriend come yet?" Daniel asked, hanging their jackets on the rack.

"She didn't say it was a date," Dad corrected.

"Peace. It was just a comment," Daniel replied without even looking at his father, as his sole presence radiated an aura of rejection Daniel couldn't stand, so he joined Mom and Yonna in the dining room.

The dining table was decorated as always. For a second, Daniel had the feeling he was a kid again. The usual red tablecloth, the floral arrangement in the center, a candle burning at each end of the table, and dishes with gold trim that Mom used on special occasions all glistened under the yellow light of the chandelier.

The bell rang and Mom went out to meet Ruth as Yonna and Daniel tried to find a place to put the presents. From the kitchen, they heard the murmur of women greeting each other. He recognized his sister's voice but wasn't sure of the third voice, so he went to greet her sister and her guest.

"Brother," announced Ruth, swaying slightly, "see whom I brought just for you." Daniel's sister gave him a hug while he held her tight or else they would have fallen on the kitchen floor. He made her sit on a chair Mom pulled up for her.

Then it was Karina's turn. She sort of jumped on Daniel's neck, and he leaned backward to distance himself a bit from the feel of her breasts on his chest. Her greeting carried a whiff of beer, which turned his stomach.

Dad came to welcome them, and Daniel ushered Yonna to the living room. "Yonna, just a warning. Ruth came with an old girlfriend of mine, and they're wasted, so don't let them push you."

"I sort of noticed," Yonna admitted, lowering her voice. "The way she threw herself all over you ..."

"Did you see her?"

"Of course," she said, crossing her arms.

"Are you really jealous?" he asked, appalled that Yonna would think he could possibly enjoy Karina's attention.

"No, but I didn't like the greeting, either."

"Karina is drunk. I'm sure tomorrow she'll dig a hole and hop in; believe me ..."

"Maybe I have a surprise for her," Yonna winked impishly.

"And what would that be?" Daniel asked, relieved that she wasn't mad at him.

"In due time," was all she said.

"Dinner is served," Mom announced from the kitchen.

When they came into the dining room, Dad was already pouring red wine into the glasses. Daniel deliberately sat in front of Yonna and by Ruth's side so that he wouldn't have to face Karina, who had no choice but to sit at the head of the table. Dad sat next to Yonna, and Mom took the other end.

Let the circus begin! Daniel thought.

Mom did not want help with the trays; within minutes, they began to engulf the duck, garnished with pears and plums, sweet potatoes, and cabbage vinaigrette.

"Daniel, aren't you goin' to introduce your wife?" Karina asked in honeyed tones.

"Yonna," he whispered to her in Spanish, "don't let her press you." He switched back to Danish and said, "Yonna, let me introduce Karina."

Yonna rose, approached Karina, and extended her hand. "Nice meeting you," she said in Danish before returning to her seat. Daniel's heart filled with pride at how Yonna handled her.

The evening went smoothly. Daniel told the group about his life in Maracaibo and how he met Yonna. He detailed how it was him who had a hard time chasing Yonna in order to extinguish any trace of hope Karina might have had regarding their past together.

They laughed and it helped relax the atmosphere. The conversation turned to Karina, then to Ruth and her photography hobby, until there was nothing left on the plates. From time to time, they could hear the noise of fireworks somewhere in the neighborhood.

Together they helped remove the plates from the table. Mom came in holding a bowl of *ris-à-l'mande*, the Christmas dessert of *risotto* with whipped cream and chopped almonds, bathed in warm cherry syrup.

Between courses, Mom told Daniel that she hoped Yonna would get the whole almond hidden in the rice so she could start the exchange of presents, but the almond landed in Ruth's portion.

Mom gave a huge package to Ruth. It was a hardcover copy of *The Art of Photography* by Bruce Barnbaum. They hugged and a very happy Ruth handed her present to Dad.

Ever since they were children, Ruth and Daniel competed to figure out the contents of the unopened presents. Judging by the shape of Ruth's gift to Dad, Daniel knew it was some music CD combo. Dad opened it without much ceremony and to his surprise, found a collection of five Anna Netrebko CDs.

Dad handed his present to Mom. There was no hug and they did not even exchange glances. She simply accepted it. Packaged beautifully with pastel wrapping paper and tiny silver stars, the gift could well be perfume, Daniel guessed. This time he was wrong—her present was cold cream.

Daniel thought that Mom was going to give him a present; instead, she approached Yonna and handed her a pink envelope. Yonna opened it. It was a picture, which she showed around, boasting a huge smile.

"Do you not know what it is?" Mom asked, now a little nervous of giving the wrong gift.

"Yes, it's a picture of a loom," Yonna replied, happy as a child.

"That is your gift but it arrives next week."

"You mean a real loom for me?" Yonna asked, eyes wide open. "I thought the present was the picture; I love it."

Yonna and Mom hugged while Dad moved around, refilling empty glasses. Katrina was reclining on the couch and toasted silently every time someone showed an opened present.

Now it was Daniel's turn. Yonna handed him a soft package wrapped in red paper with Christmas trees printed on it, exchanging knowing looks with Mom. He shook it, with the hope that the noise would betray what was inside. He concluded that it must be a trendy pair of boxers in lively colors. His family circle closed in around him, giving the impression that only Daniel was not part of the secret shared by the rest of them.

He opened the gift carefully. It was a white garment, and Daniel started to shake when he realized it was a tiny white top with a matching pant set. A pacifier was on top. He looked up at Yonna to make sure it was not a joke.

"We're pregnant," she confirmed.

All except for one broke into applause.

Chapter

35

(2010)

THANKS TO THE loom Anne-Marie gave me, I filled the hours making rugs to distract myself from the weather. It was not the cold that tormented me. My problem was the dim daylight, as if the sun refused to rise.

I usually went for a walk in the woods before I started weaving. The chill breeze cleared my thoughts as I enjoyed the sight of the tiny white flowers bursting everywhere. They reminded me of *jeyutse*, the white verbena.

"Those are wood anemone, typical of early spring," Daniel explained.

During those walks, I would dwell on the idea of starting my own business as Thea did in Maracaibo. It made much more sense to me than sending letter after letter of job applications that would simply be rejected. One of the most common reasons companies gave me was that I didn't speak Danish very well, which was true to an extent. Another reason was that I didn't have much experience in the field, even when it came to cleaning. Did I really need professional training to mop the floors and keep a shop tidy?

Either way, the pregnancy had forced me to take a break from the job search. No one would be willing to pay maternity leave for a worker who had just arrived.

I called Thea whenever I could, and she wept with joy when I told her we were expecting twins. I thought that would encourage her to visit us but she felt too old to sit on a plane. To worsen matters, we couldn't fly since I was due in four weeks.

I sensed that Thea wasn't telling me everything about her health; the last time I phoned, one of the *Zapuanas* told me she wasn't all right. I tried to discuss the issue with her.

"*Liebe*, I'm just an old woman; I'm fine," she dismissed my concerns.

The saying "a half-loaf is better than none" couldn't be more true. I missed Thea and her Spanish tinted with a German accent, but Anne-Marie compensated for her just fine. She came over almost every day.

"Yonna, I think you should start your own business," Anne-Marie advised every time we talked. "I'm willing to help you with the contacts, organizing exhibitions, and administrative assistance."

In part, I knew she genuinely wanted to help, but I also knew that Anne-Marie wanted to stay as far from her husband as possible. She did very little to conceal the fact that they were two strangers living under the same roof.

Matters worsened at an Easter lunch Anne-Marie arranged for us. I noticed that the old man was grouchier than usual. He didn't utter a word, grumbling something no one could hear, but I'd learned to ignore his sinister humor.

At some point, Anne-Marie needed help to fetch cold soft drinks from a chest fridge they had in the tool shed, so I volunteered to bring them. I was busy putting the bottles in a bag Anne-Marie gave me to carry the bottles, when Daniel's dad scared me by standing in the doorway. I sort of jumped back at the sight. He laughed as he asked, "Do you know what horny means?"

"Sorry, I didn't hear you," I said, not sure if I understood.

"Horny," he replied, now rubbing his crotch.

I felt a wave of rage warming up my ears. No pain, no fear, just this growing raw rage. I ignored the fact that he was rubbing between his legs and grabbed one of the bottles I just put in the bag.

"I guess that's slang for sick bastard," I shot back, holding his gaze.

I'm not afraid of you, you piece of trash, I thought.

"I know you've got plenty of dick ... I heard Daniel and Anne-Marie's chat about it the other day," he retorted, leaning forward.

"You slimy puke," I snapped, as I wielded the bottle like a sword on my way out. He stepped aside with raised hands, as if I was pointing a gun at him.

I walked the path back to the house, unafraid of the man I left behind, with the freeing sensation that men like him would no longer be able to hurt me.

I headed for the kitchen and found Anne-Marie staring at me with a contorted face, but she said nothing. It was tough to say if she witnessed what her husband did.

"Are you okay?" Daniel asked me when he saw my flushed cheeks.

"I've never been better," I said, picking a bite of fish.

We sat around the table, and Daniel's dad joined us as if nothing happened. His lack of shame was disturbing. That man wasn't well.

"What are you waiting for to take a test?" he asked Daniel.

"Test for what?" Daniel asked, puzzled.

"DNA. How do you know those kids are yours?" he snapped, with his mouth filled with fish.

I stopped chewing and begged *Mareygua*, the supreme God. *He'll soon say it's a bad joke*, I thought, but it never happened.

"Listen, you piece of shit," Daniel said, grabbing his dad by the lapels. "We only *endure* you because of that woman over there," he paused, looking over at Anne-Marie, "but the day you guys get divorced, I will not even bother to go to your funeral."

"Daniel, stop," Anne-Marie and I pleaded near hysterically.

Daniel released his father, who almost rolled down to the floor with the chair.

"My, my, what a temper," he muttered as he regained his balance. Apart from the red face and bloodshot eyes, he remained calm but challenging.

"Please, let's be civil," Anne-Marie pleaded in a vain attempt to get things back to the bearable state they had been in for such a long time, but Daniel didn't seem to let it go.

"Depraved shit," Daniel shouted as he took me by the arm and almost dragged me out of the house.

Anne-Marie followed us to the door with the saddest face I had ever seen on anyone.

When I next saw her during a visit a few days later, over a cup of coffee, she told me, "Yonna, I owe you an explanation. We married not long after we met. He insisted that I didn't need to work as he earned more than enough. I truly regret it because I never learned a trade. I devoted my time to our home, taking care of Daniel and Ruth, and becoming a good hostess.

"The problems started when Daniel was born. The old man never got over the fact that Daniel didn't resemble him. Although he never abused him, he never took him to baseball matches, no fishing, no camping, no good-night reading, or playing at all. It was hard for Daniel to witness how devoted he was to Ruth.

"I guess Daniel preferred to swallow the humiliation and avoid conflict, but as he grew, he got tired of waiting for his father's approval. He began to confront him more openly, to such an extent that things were nearly out of hand.

"When they were small, we had to endure the bitter pill of the grumpy old man. His tactic was simple but effective: if he was in a bad mood, he came home, slammed doors, and didn't talk to anyone. He would lock himself in his study, keeping the rest of the family at bay for days. If I needed money, I had to report in detail what it would be used for and return what I did not manage to spend. On top of it, the other women …

"For him, it was not enough to have sex with them; he made sure that common friends saw him. I became his clown. He was so sure that I wouldn't leave him because, after all, where would I go if I couldn't stand up for myself?" Tears rolled down Anne-Marie's cheeks.

"I know he's made a pass at you, too ..."

I tried to comfort her but she only wanted to vent years of repressed frustration. "I'm okay, Yonna, really. I just need to talk," she assured me between sobs.

"But he was good to Ruth, wasn't he?" I dared to ask.
"Yes, but Daniel is his son, too."

Chapter

36

(2011)

"WHAT DO YOU think of me and your mom as business partners?" I asked Daniel as we were lying in bed.

"Mmm, I think it's a good idea, but be careful. She can be a little bit too much," he warned me between kisses.

"How?" I managed to ask.

"Well, you know ... She might end up running the whole show. Sometimes she reminds me of Thea," Daniel confessed.

"As long as I have freedom to weave my rugs, I don't mind her deciding on everything else," I assured him. "You know, I'm not good at running businesses, and money in my hands is like water down the sewer. Your mom really fell into my lap and it seems she has all the skills I'll never have."

I have a hunch that Anne-Marie wanted to start her own project. She wanted to build something from scratch on her own to show her husband that she too could start things. Anne-Marie was in a hurry. She wanted to start as soon as possible, anticipating that once I had the twins, things would slow down for a while.

We tried to find a place for the business and actually saw three sites that could have been perfect but were over our budget. We tagged the issue as a small defeat and instead decided to take another approach— present the rugs at craft shows. From her years as a hostess, Anne-Marie knew many people and some of them owed her a favor or two. After a few phone calls and half a dozen emails, the library in Hilleroed gave us the opportunity to show a selection of ten carpets.

It was good news but it also made us work at a forced march, as we had to label the items, prepare brochures and stationery, and transport and set up the entire display.

The library staff were simply amazing. They helped us in every way they could. Anne-Marie assisted me in selecting pieces for the show. There were items I had made in Maracaibo, patterns depicting the sun, the moon, eclipses, peacocks, and the Garden of Eden.

A day before the exhibition, we managed to arrange everything at the library and headed home to celebrate our first victory. We had dinner at our place. Ruth popped by to say hello and wished us the best of luck. I could easily spot the stunning resemblance between her and her father. The thin lips, the slightly short, turned-up nose, the spare lashes she thickened with a layer of mascara. I didn't notice all this before, as we never became the best of friends; those details about her sharpened after my mother-in-law's confession.

Daniel and Anne-Marie toasted on my behalf, since I didn't dare drink alcohol.

At the end of the evening, Anne-Marie went home. I was so exhausted that I slipped into bed early and fell asleep praying to *Mareygua* for a good day at the show.

Violent contractions awoke me at midnight. I crawled out of bed, trying not to make any noise, but I heard a pop, and warm fluid gushed between my legs. Daniel woke up and we realized that I was going to give birth soon.

Daniel didn't want to take any risks so we rode to the hospital by taxi. Upon arrival, it all happened like a whirlwind. The ultrasound showed that one of the twins had an umbilical cord wrapped around his neck. This, coupled with the fact that my water had already broken, led the doctors to a quick decision to perform an emergency C-section.

With Selma, everything went smoothly, but Tobias took a bit longer due to the tangled umbilical cord. Other than that, we were okay. The two babies slept in their cribs while I recovered in bed. It was a relief that in the end, everything worked with little Tobias, as it felt like an eternity to take him out of my belly. A sinking feeling was starting to settle in both Daniel and me, when the doctors announced that the baby was well. Daniel didn't say much but his stern expression and wet eyes told me books about his state of mind. He was happy beyond words yet he didn't know how to express it.

"What did you do to speed up labor?" the doctor asked.

"We've been working on an exhibition show. I weave rugs and I guess we just got carried away ..."

"Well, I guess you'll miss the show this time," he said, gently patting my arm. "You have to stay here for a few days."

Anne-Marie came to visit us at the hospital and suggested canceling the whole exhibition show, since she rather wanted to be together with us.

"Nonsense," I told her in my bad Danish, which made her burst out laughing. "We've been working so hard for this moment, so we cannot waste this opportunity," I assured her.

She took my advice reluctantly and after the exhibition, she reported to me.

"Yonna, everyone was interested in the eclipse," she said as she rummaged in her bag to pull out a couple of business cards. "See, these two are very interested in your technique, and it does not end there. Do you remember Ms. Frederiksen, the retired nurse?" my mother-in-law asked solemnly.

Our watchful neighbor, I thought. I looked over Anne-Marie's shoulder and spotted Daniel, busying himself with the babies.

"She is very interested in your rugs and offered to give a helping hand with whatever we might need."

"That's very kind of her," said Daniel, with a touch of surprise.

I nodded in agreement. "She's welcome to."

I was too tired to deal with the issues of our business. *That can wait,* I thought with a hint of nostalgia. When Anne-Marie mentioned the

151

eclipse, it reminded me of Thea. I wished she were there, with her red cheeks, full of energy, giving orders, and taking care of everything. I promised myself to call her once we were back home.

"There's something else," she said with hesitation. "I've found an apartment not far from here."

"We can discuss it when we leave the hospital," I managed to say.

"It's not for the business ... I left your father," Anne-Marie explained, looking at Daniel.

I froze and Daniel left the babies in their cribs to hug his mother.

We came back home after five days at the hospital. Aside from the curtains in the twins' bedroom, everything was in place. The green walls made the room a little too dark, so I solved the problem by gluing white paper doves to the walls with Anne-Marie's help. Daniel wasn't sure at the beginning but was truly happy when he saw the birds arranged as if they had flown in through the window and spread over the walls. Daniel assembled the white cribs and they stood facing each other, the changing table between them. Anne-Marie took me to a secondhand store where I found a lamp resembling a white cloud and we finished the work with two mats I had woven depicting *senkeyuu*, the twins.

The twins gave me a full plate. There were days when I didn't even manage to brush my teeth. I could have taken naps when Selma and Tobias slept, but doing so would have meant neglecting our home.

The first month and a half passed and I realized I hadn't phoned Thea. A feeling of shame came over me, so I grabbed the phone and placed a call directly to the craft shop. Thea picked up and I broke into tears when I heard her voice.

"*Verdammt!* Is Daniel misbehaving?" she barked over the line.

"No, Thea. I'm crying because I gave birth a month ago, and I've been so busy that I haven't had time to call you."

"Oh, you scared me, child. I thought Daniel was taking a wrong course," she said hoarsely. "God bless you, dear; how are the little treasures doing?"

"They're all right but I'm tired. We don't sleep much at night. Yesterday

I breastfed Selma twice by mistake, and poor Tobias had to settle for a feeding bottle."

"You need to rest, even if the house falls apart," Thea advised. "If they are over a month old, that means they arrived earlier than expected, doesn't it?"

"Yes, by three weeks. I guess I worked too hard for an exhibition show and that sped up the whole thing."

"Are you exhibiting your rugs?" Thea asked. I detected a trace of exhaustion in her voice.

"Yes, thanks to Daniel's mother Anne-Marie, my business partner. There is another woman who also wants to join us."

"Congratulations, dear. I'm happy for you, really." She paused, then added, "You're not planning to come to Maracaibo soon, are you?"

"Of course, we want you to meet Selma and Tobias, but the doctor advised us to wait until they're three months old, something to do with the cabin air pressure and their ears. How are you?" I asked.

"My liver is bothering me, old people stuff, you know ..."

"Your liver?" I repeated, not knowing what to say. "Does it hurt?"

"Not at all, I'm just tired. The doctor prescribed some vitamins."

"Sure it's nothing serious?" I insisted.

"*Liebe*, I have to go; a customer just came in," Thea announced. "Come soon, please."

"Send our greetings to the *Zapuanas*," I managed to say. When Thea hung up, I realized that I didn't hear the bell ringing in the background, like I normally would.

Daniel's expression when I told him about Thea's liver brought a premonition. I couldn't stop thinking about *epieyu*, the flying vulture carrying the essence of the dead in his beak.

Chapter

37

(2012)

THE PHONE RANG at nine in the morning here in Denmark, and when I heard the *Zapuana*, I knew.

Thea had died in her bed, quietly, smiling, sure of having fulfilled her mission in this world. Those were her last words, the *Zapuana* said. She also told me that Thea left an envelope for me, which I would have to pick up in person.

It was sheer bad luck as we had already bought the flight tickets and had planned to leave in a week and a half. Once again, I was away. I'd been absent when my people were killed, and now absent at Thea's death.

I phoned Daniel at his office and he knew immediately that something was wrong. I never called when he was at work.

"Thea …" was all I managed to say with a broken voice.

"I'm so sorry to hear that, Yonna."

"We must advance the trip," I said after a pause.

Anne-Marie and Ms. Frederiksen offered to take care of Tobias and Selma, as this was no longer a social trip but to take care of a burial.

When we finally arrived at the house of a thousand colors on Santa Lucia Street, it seemed unreal that Thea's vitality was gone. The house looked the same, but despite the neatness, a ghostly chill made my blood run cold. *The vacuum left by death*, I figured.

155

Liebe Yonna,

If you are reading this letter, it is because it was too late. Do not blame yourself; there is no reason to feel guilty. In my heart, you were always present.

Liebe Yonna, you were the daughter I wish I had given to Gualtiero. My heart was here in Maracaibo because of him, so please make sure that my remains are cremated.

The other day, I saw on the news cows grazing in the cemetery, eating wreaths. There were also open tombs with skulls exposed. I want you to be present the day my ashes fall into Gualtiero's grave because I do not want my bones at the mercy of crooks.

Regarding my money, it's yours, apart from a small amount I have assigned to the Zapuanas. You've earned it with hard work. The lawyer took care of it.

I am pleased to know that Anne-Marie is your partner, for your detachment from material things makes you an awful businesswoman. I know that she and Daniel will help you make good decisions, so listen to their advice.

The only thing I regret is not having the opportunity to meet Selma and Tobias, but I know they are in good hands. Give them my blessings.

Please tell Daniel that my promise still stands if he ever hurts you. He knows what I am talking about.

Liebe Yonna, you should know that there is another reason why I never went back to Germany. When I met Gualtiero, it was through my sister, who was his fiancée. The marriage never took place because we ran away. That's how we ended up in Maracaibo. You see? I too have my sins.

I became a renegade for what I did to my sister, but it was liberating to know that I did not want to be elsewhere—only with Gualtiero. When I buried him, I realized that my country was no longer where I was born, but where I put my heart.

Liebe Yonna, thanks for your company and for your loyalty. I know we will meet someday in eternity.

God bless you.
Dorothea Weiss

Daniel and I read the letter in silence and made all the arrangements to execute her last will.

"These cemetery things remind me of my dad. He dreams of a flashy burial, as if he has made great contributions to humanity," Daniel said with a wry chuckle.

I grimaced at the idea, and all that Anne-Marie told me about her marriage came to mind.

"I guess you want to be buried here in Maracaibo," he ventured, bringing me back to the present. The statement surprised me because I had never thought of where I wanted to be put to rest. Death became distant for someone who had survived so much misery. *I can't possibly have a short life*, I thought.

"When I lost my family, I felt I belonged nowhere, then you, Daniel, came along, and Selma and Tobias."
Daniel stopped short and hugged me hard. "Let's go home," he whispered.

Taraji

Chapter

38

(1997)
Soweto, South Africa

SINCE THE ASSAULT, she had not dared to go out, especially for the last three months. She did not want the neighbors to see her belly. *Why did I have to leave the house and buy kerosene?* she thought.

If I had stayed home ...

She asked the night why, but all she heard were gunshots in some distant place and fear struck her once again. She sometimes asked Mam' Akindi the same question, but "You're alive, my dear" was the only answer she gave her.

She was scared to be alone and now the pressure in her belly woke her up. First, she thought it was a dream, yet her belly tightened and sent waves of spasms down her body. The baby wanted out; the time had come. She could tell because she had never felt this recurring throbbing before—like two giant hands gripping each side of her belly and pushing, pushing down.

The fear grew inside her when she remembered the elder's words describing the excruciating pain that came with each contraction. Mam' Akindi gave birth to eight children, and she herself witnessed the delivery of the last three of her brothers. This reminded her of Mam' Akindi's labor pains ...

She was alone. After the assault, Mam' Akindi and her brothers volunteered to patrol around the train station.

If she asked the neighbors for help, the news would spread and she did not want that.

Ahhh!

She couldn't stop picturing Mam' Akindi's last delivery. She recalled how her mother scolded herself whenever a cry escaped her.

I'd better stand up, she thought. The pain was suffocating her. Sweat ran down her back, as she remembered the only toy she ever had: a bicycle wheel she guided around with a dead branch. The rain fell on her back then, like the sweat drops running now.

The only thing that covered her body in those days was a pink hipster with lots of frills on it, which resembled a cauliflower. She was just a little girl, but this was a happy memory she cherished to help her hold on.

She tried to go to the backyard for some fresh air, but she couldn't control the trembling of her legs as she felt the pressure in her belly, like something inside her was going to break down into small pieces. She managed to rise to her feet, although she noticed the warmth of something watery running down her thighs. When she touched it, she realized she had peed all over herself.

She could hear the timbals in Kaapse Klopse inside her chest. She pushed by instinct, even though she did not want to. She reached out to hold on to something that would keep her from falling as the inner voices chanted, *push, push*.

In one swift move, she took off the soaked, large T-shirt and bent forward to push again. This time, a stream of jelly gushed down, like water being poured from a bucket. She did not dare to kneel for fear of being unable to get to her feet again. She tried her best to swallow the pain, while warm tears soaked her face.

Instinct took over.

"Ohhhh," she moaned.

Down there, something was stretching and burning, as if she were sitting by the campfire where Mam' Akindi burned the trash.

She put her hands right there where she peed and felt the baby's head. She thought no longer; the baby was coming. She knew that when the baby was out of her guts, there would be no more pain. She had to pull out the baby, no matter what. *Come out, out* ... she repeated the words silently a thousand times, desperate to ease the pain and to help the baby be born. *Push! Push!*

"Ahhhh!" she cried out, feeling tingling cramps in her legs as she rested both hands on her knees. Her belly rose and fell in pace with the spasms while threads of slime hung from her buttocks like pendulums. *Now I can feel the baby's head,* she thought, filled with hope that soon all would be over.

Even though the pain became less strong, the cramps urged her to push again, as she prepared to catch the little body. One last push, a gentle pull, and the little body was in her hands.

She knelt for the first time with the baby in her arms and heard her cry. It was more like a squeak of a baby bird. She began to cover the baby with the T-shirt she took off moments ago, as Mam' Mirembe, the neighbor, entered the house.

Mam' Mirembe ran to her when she saw her kneeling, holding the baby.

"God's child, let me help ye," the old woman said.

With expert hands, she cut the umbilical cord and swaddled the baby with the first piece of fabric she found.

"It's a secret," she told the woman, in tears, still panting. "Mam' Mirembe, promise me you won't tell anyone."

"Mam' Akindi told me to keep an eye on ye, child. We must find a midwife or take ye to the hospital, ye hasn't dropped the cake yet. Ye're gonna be sick."

"Cake?"

"Yes, it's like a second birth, but no pain. If ye don't get it out, ye'll be sick. That stuff rots in yer guts," Mam' Mirembe said as she put the little bundle in her arms. "But she's fine."

"She?"

"Yeah, it's a girl."

Chapter

39

(1997)
Soweto, South Africa

MAM' AKINDI SAT, playing with the baby on her lap as she waited for Mam' Dikeledi. Next to the chair where she sat, she had put down on the floor the bag with the few baby's clothes she brought with her. Apart from the blanket Mam' Mirembe had given her daughter the day she found her giving birth on the living room floor, the rest was old stuff her own children had worn when they were small.

She'd felt a twinge of shame when forced to explain the circumstances of her daughter's pregnancy to Mam' Mirembe, but she needed someone close enough to keep an eye on her daughter while they all were away patrolling near the train station.

Not that Mam' Mirembe had requested any explanation. Mam' Mirembe was a compassionate, good woman who never engaged in gossip; she was known for having a heart of gold, and as a good woman, she promised not to repeat what she saw.

With the bundle cradled in her arms, Mam' Akindi observed her surroundings. The waiting room was a porch with chairs and a table covered with a plastic tablecloth, placed by the window. On the table there was a water jug with ice cubes and a tower of plastic cups, right next to the door leading to the old house.

The bundle resting on her lap began to move. Suddenly, the little girl managed to take her little arms out of the blanket and began to examine her own fingers. Mam' Akindi smiled with surprise at the precocity of the girl.

"You're going to be an inquisitive little woman, aren't you? You're only two days old and you have found your hands," she whispered to the baby.

The steps of a woman—who apparently was Mam' Dikeledi—made her raise her gaze.

"Welcome, Mam' Akindi, my name is Dikeledi," she said, extending her arm.

Mam' Akindi nodded, showing a toothless smile.

"Please come with me," Mam' Dikeledi added, leading Mam' Akindi down a corridor only lit by the light entering through the perforated blocks. In the background, she could hear children playing in what seemed to be the house's backyard.

On their way, Mam' Akindi studied what was about to become her granddaughter's new home. At the end of the hall was an office with pale yellow walls. There were a desk and a metal filing cabinet with a fan on top, working unceasingly.

Mam' Dikeledi closed the door as she beckoned Mam' Akindi to sit on the chair.

"I guess you have come because of the baby, haven't you?"

"Yes, my daughter can't take care of her. I thought that the best way to help this girl is to put her in a place like this."

"Your daughter?" inquired Mam' Dikeledi. "Why didn't she come herself?"

"She was assaulted one evening when she went out to buy kerosene ..." Mam' Akindi said, pursing her lips.

"Oh, I see, I'm sorry."

"I'm very sorry, too," said Mam' Akindi, lowering her head. It revived the images of her daughter's appearance when they found her. *How do you report the case to a police department that doesn't even dare to patrol in Kliptown?*

Mam' Dikeledi interrupted Mam' Akindi's thoughts. "The procedure is very simple," she said. "First, write down all the information about the child so we can start the process. This doesn't mean she's given up for adoption immediately because we have to run blood tests to rule out HIV and hepatitis. Sometimes, the parents are involved in the adoption process."

"How?"

"Well, I mean the parents help us choose the most appropriate candidates for the baby."

"Not us," said Mam' Akindi, dismissing the idea. "My daughter doesn't want any contact with the baby. See, she is very young and has so much to heal."

"I understand," said Mam' Dikeledi, studying Mam' Akindi above the rim of her glasses. "Then there isn't much to say. There are some papers you have to sign and you must hand over the girl, but please note that once you have delivered the documents, there is no turning back."

"Signing? I can't write. It's very little what people like me can do. We know it's going to rain because of the smell of wet earth, and when it rains in Kliptown, the raindrops don't fall from the sky; the water pours out of the houses. We know it is night because it's pitch black, and the difference between the blue night and the black night is that in the blue night, the sky is filled with stars and hope beats in our hearts. The black night is different ... My daughter felt the black night," Mam' Akindi said with wet eyes.

"I didn't want to put you down by assuming you couldn't read, Mam' Akindi," replied Mam' Dikeledi, lowering her eyes and admonishing herself for the blunder.

Mam' Akindi was not used to reaping anything good from life. There was outright resignation in what came out of her mouth, resignation and pain.

"Does—does the baby have a name?" Mam' Dikeledi dared to ask.

"No name, but I'd like her to be called Taraji."

"Taraji," repeated Mam' Dikeledi. "It's a pretty name; do you know what Taraji means?"

"It means hope; I wish that Taraji only sees the blue night," said the old woman as she handed the baby to Mam' Dikeledi.

Chapter

40

JACOB
(2002)
Farum - Denmark

JACOB GOT OFF the car at full speed and glanced back at the old Volvo 740 to make sure he had parked it well aligned to the left, as he didn't want to hear Mrs. Frederiksen bitching about his shitty parking and the narrowness of the alley.

That would explain why Peter never visits her, he thought.

Liva had phoned and urgently asked him to come, without giving details. Jacob quickened his pace toward the house through the trail of stones leading up to the kitchen door. He pushed the hose Liva used to water the garden. She forgot to put it in place that morning or Carson played with it, he hypothesized while he snuck into the house.

He opened the door and found his wife sitting in the kitchen with a cup of tea and red, swollen eyes, holding a sheet of paper. Carson greeted him, wagging his tail.

"What happened?" he asked, putting the car keys on the tabletop.

"Nothing's wrong, love; I'm crying from mere joy."

"But when you called me you sounded as if—as if something terrible had happened. Why didn't you explain it before I left?"

Liva handed him a sheet of paper, ignoring his comment.

As he read, his eyes filled with tears, too. It was an email from the adoption agency.

Mr. Jacob and Mrs. Liva Ravn
Bakkevej 11
3520 Farum
Denmark

Johannesburg, January 25, 2002

Reference is made to case No. 16387526. After having considered the application for adoption and its enclosures submitted by you on August 28, 2001, it is our pleasure to inform you that you have been approved by this office as noted in the meeting of January 20, 2002.

In accordance with our internal rules, and taking our practice concerning the applicant's age into consideration, we have great pleasure to inform you that we have a suitable candidate. Her name is Taraji, a five-year-old girl in perfect health who is in need of a loving home. Therefore, we would like to present her for your kind consideration as she matches in age with your profile.

In case you do not agree with this suggestion, kindly let us know as soon as possible.

Warmest regards,

Parents of the Sacred Heart Adoption Agency

"This calls for a beer," he managed to say.

Liva stood and hugged him while Carson, panting, watched them.

"Congratulations, now you can call yourself Dad," announced Liva, giving him a quick kiss on the lips.

Jacob held her tightly as his face disappeared in her hair. He lifted his wife by the hips and spun her around the kitchen.

"Watch out, you crazy," he heard her say. Carson was now barking. He put her down, exhausted, which reminded him how out of shape he was.

"Congratulations, Mom," he whispered with a broken voice.

"It's incredible that we're just one step away from having our daughter. Our daughter, Jacob!"

"Yeah," he agreed as she twirled with joy.

Liva was a good planner and she wanted to start right away. Jacob understood her, since it had been nearly three years since they submitted the first application. Apparently, they were nearly at the end of a long road.

They sent the first application and had to wait for a social worker; after countless home visits, the tests, the assessment, the report of the social worker and the scrutiny of their finances, were they good enough as parents? Yes, they were. Were they stable enough for the challenge of raising an adoptive child? Yes, they were. There were more assessments, the list, the short-listing, and the final approval in South Africa.

Liva showed Jacob the list of things to do that she had written while waiting for him. He had no other option but to admire her; her persistence had once again paid off.

THANKS TO THE YELLOW pamphlet, Liva and Jacob were happily married. Laurits and Rasmus also had their share of responsibility in the matter. They were tired of the fact that Jacob's nose was buried in books and that they didn't have records of his romantic escapades so far, so they dragged him to the Roskilde Festival in 1984.

Rasmus put the pamphlet on the table where Jacob was having lunch in the faculty canteen and announced that he was on a mission to keep him away from books, if only for six days. Rasmus said he was truly concerned that time was passing and Jacob was going to remain a virgin.

Jacob thought it was a joke. He took the piece of paper. It was a snapshot of an orange circus tent, surrounded by a field of yellow flowers. Below the picture, there was information on the festival's dates, written in matching colors. Farther down, the list of the bands: Lou Reed, Paul Young, Gnags, and TV-2; the print became smaller, stating the lesser-known bands.

"Here," said Rasmus, laying the ticket on the table. "Laurits and I bought it for you, so you don't have any excuses."

"You bastards," Jacob said as he gave him a hug. "All right, I'll go with you guys; the beers are on me."

They embarked on a six-day journey of beer, rock, pop, and mud. As it happened, Laurits and Rasmus were drunk before, during, and after the festival.

On his own, Jacob went to listen to Gnags, since Laurits and Rasmus were sleeping off the hangover from the night before. Apparently, they had forgotten the mission to help him lose his virginity. The atmosphere was amazing: people dancing, the smell of sweaty bodies after so many days without a shower, and the smell of beer all intermingled. Nobody cared, since that was the very soul of the festival.

The lyrics of *"Slingrer ned ad Vestergade"* could be heard from where he was standing. He approached the stage. The night was navy blue, and the raised arms of the audience were like a bamboo forest swaying gently in the wind.

There she was, listening to the music with an expression of pure rapture on her face. Jacob felt the same rapture observing her. Brown locks fell over her bare shoulders; she was wearing a light dress with tiny flowers, which made him lose track of time. Jacob didn't realize the song had ended, and she approached him.

"Hello."

No way. These things simply don't happen to me, he thought. *It's not me.*

Jacob turned to look at the face of the lucky guy.

"It's you," she said, laughing as she reached out her hand to greet him. "My name is Liva."

"Jacob," he managed to say through a dry mouth.

He couldn't believe his luck, as he counted the seconds before she would run off bored.

Many say that when lacking the looks, you'd better have the gift of gab.

Liva told him about her life and her dreams. He must have asked the right questions because they talked all night. Jacob said very little about himself. All he wanted was to know everything about her, to hear her talking. He could have become a giant pair of ears with two eyes in between, just to admire her beautiful brown eyes and the casual way she kept flicking the hair from her shoulders.

He was glad that she, too, lived in Copenhagen. She was studying design, her idol was some guy named David Carson, and she wanted to see the world. They gave each other awkward kisses that tasted of beer and sausages and toasts and glory. They made love in the first tent they found available.

Rasmus and Laurits resented his absence.

As far as Jacob was concerned, he thought Liva would disappear when the fumes of the beers they drank had evaporated. This one-night stand was something she would tell her friends about as part of what happened at a festival. In that, too, Jacob was wrong. The next weekend they met, and the next, and the next again. He hardly slept on campus.

"Liva and I moved in together," he had announced to his friends over one of those Friday beers, and they seemed happy on Jacob's behalf, but little by little they drifted apart.

Liva and Jacob agreed to take a six-month break from university to experience other cultures, feel the world in the first person. They saw the sacred Ganges River, ate *kothu roti* on the streets of Colombo, dove in Sihanoukville, enjoyed the view of the Grand Palace in Bangkok, and admired the Po Nagar towers near the town of Nha Trang. The only luggage they carried was what they could fit in their backpacks.

When they returned to Denmark, they graduated, started working, and fourteen years passed, just like blowing the flame of a candle.

Jacob popped the question and Liva accepted on the condition that before jumping into the world of adults (despite both having passed their thirties), they should celebrate where it all started: Roskilde Festival, but this time it was edition 1998.

Unfortunately, Gnags and TV-2 were replaced by Kraftwerk, Black Sabbath, Oscar D' Leon, and D.A.D.

The festival was memorable since they crossed a few boundaries: they drunk a lot, again. They made love in random tents, again. They danced salsa for the first time ever, and Liva and Jacob ran in the festival's first naked race. That was how they prepared to settle down and start a family.

Chapter

41

JACOB

AFTER A STOPOVER in Zurich and the ten-and-a-half-hour flight, Jacob and Liva arrived at O.R. Tambo International Airport in Johannesburg. They had never been to South Africa before; it was time to pick up their daughter, Taraji.

They had not had the opportunity to enjoy her in pictures, yet they talked about her like she had been a part of the family since birth.

When Jacob thought back, he honestly felt sorry for Liva and the countless nights she cried when her menstruation came. It was like with every bleeding, her heart bled dry, too, and he'd agreed to the adoption because it was her idea. Jacob himself would not have dared to suggest it, since he did not want her to feel like they had to have kids no matter what, but he was glad she insisted.

"What if Taraji doesn't want to come with us?" Liva asked with a worried expression.

"Don't worry; everything's going to be just fine. Besides, we will stay here long enough to find out. She will accept us; you'll see ..." Jacob reassured her, even though doubts tormented him, too.

"Yes, you're right," said Liva, watching out of the window. "We don't need to be worried."

Suddenly, the traffic slowed and he could see on the sidewalk across the street a barber cutting a young man's hair. He had just finished and the client was checking the results from a broken mirror the barber was holding.

How different things are on this side of the world, he pondered, as they moved slowly in the traffic.

The taxi driver pulled in front of the hotel on Jones Road and got off the car to help them with their luggage. They paid him; the driver wished them luck as he drove away into the bustle of the city.

Once they were up in their room, while Liva splashed her face with water, Jacob managed to find the phone number to call the agency.

For a three-star hotel, the room was lavish. There was a double bed with white bedding and perfectly folded green sheets across the bed, and two sets of pillows on top. The back wall boasted the silhouette of a naked couple on a pale green background. Jacob opened the window; deafening noise from the streets and a puff of car exhaust reminded him of where they were.

After reporting their arrival to the agency, they agreed to meet in one hour.

They took another cab to the agency to meet the contact, who would take them to the orphanage. When they arrived, a short man was waiting for them in front of the building. Orange patches of moisture had seized the front walls.

The man beckoned them to follow him through a narrow gate, which led to an iron door and a closed passage. The man made them sit in a waiting room with orange curtains and dark brown chairs.

Liva and Jacob did not exchange a word, as they were alert to every sound.

A large woman in a light red dress, her head wrapped in a shiny green turban, welcomed them with a magnificent smile.

"Welcome and my apologies for making you wait. My name is Bahati," she said as they shook hands. "Would you like a cup of tea?"

"A glass of water would be enough," Jacob said and Liva agreed.

The lady beckoned the man, who had received them at the entrance, to fetch water. He relayed the order to a third person whom Liva and Jacob could not see from where they were sitting.

"You are Taraji's parents, aren't you?" she asked, smiling.

"Yes," replied Liva, smiling back while Jacob was sorting through the documents they would have to show.

"May I have the documents?"

"Sure, I just have to separate the originals from the copies," said Jacob, concentrating on the papers.

The man came back with the water.

"Everything is in a manila folder," Jacob announced as he handed her the sheaf of documents he fastened with a paperclip.

Mam' Bahati leafed through and apparently everything was in order, since she nodded.

"Well, if you have no objection, I think it's time to meet the girl," she declared.

Chapter

42

LIVA

ON THEIR WAY to the orphanage, Mercy May, both Liva and Jacob could appreciate the reality of poverty in Soweto. The cab drove in many areas where the roads were nonexistent. There were all kinds of stalls on both sides of the streets and hills of trash piled everywhere, at the disposal of goats, stray dogs, and vultures alike.

This brought her back to their backpack trip to Varanasi, when she and Jacob went to experience the sacred river.

Even though she had nothing but endearing recollections of that trip and still cherished the memory of beautiful sunsets over the Ganges, the amazing energy and spiritual awareness it aroused, she also recalled the stench of feces, to such an extent that it assaulted her senses.

In a way, she was mentally prepared for something similar here in Soweto. Here it smelled dusty but mostly of smog.

Smog is the smell of Soweto, she thought.

Liva gazed back and all she saw were some children playing street football in the reddish cloud of dust the taxi left behind. They drove past a black-and-white sign saying, "Welcome to Soweto." At a distance, she spotted the towers of the old power station and pointed in that direction for Jacob to see.

"That's the Orlando Power Station," the taxi driver said. "It's for electricity in Johannesburg but they don't work anymore."

"Johannesburg? What about Soweto?" Liva asked, puzzled, moving

177

forward to hear what the driver was saying.

"Not Soweto. The electric power is too expensive for most of us. The towers are here but they were intended to supply power to Johannesburg."

Liva didn't know what to say, so she nodded at him and leaned back on the seat.

"I read the other day in the newspaper about someone complaining about a chimney spoiling his view," she whispered in Danish to Jacob.

"Shame on us," Jacob replied. "We are so privileged; on top of that, we still dare to whine."

Liva nodded and studied the changing landscape through the window.

"This must be it," the driver announced, stopping in front of a green house.

A blue, grilled fence surrounded Mercy May. Two ladies, who appeared to be twins, stood waiting.

"Welcome to Mercy May; my name is Candis and she is Mam' Dede," said one of the women as Jacob and Liva approached.

"How was your trip?" Mam' Dede asked.

"Fine, it's our first time but surely will not be the last," Liva said, extending her hand to greet the two women.

After the greetings, they entered a room with dark blue curtains. In the background, there was a bookcase showing what seemed to be trophies. At the bottom of the bookcase were two rows of cardboard boxes, stacked on top of each other. In front of the boxes, there were three white plastic chairs. The laughter of playing children drifted through the air.

"Would you like to have a cup of tea or would you prefer coffee?" asked Mam' Dede.

"Tea would be fine," Liva replied.

"We are well aware that you are eager to meet Taraji," said Mam' Candis. "But it would be good for you to understand the process to make the handover as smooth as possible."

Liva and Jacob rushed to agree, afraid of giving the impression that they would run to the airport immediately after they received Taraji.

"A cup of tea for me would be fine," Liva repeated.

"Me, too," added Jacob, taking Liva's hand reassuringly.

Mam' Candis left the room to prepare the tea.

"The first meetings with Taraji will be observed," said Mam' Dede. "Preferably short visits."

She hesitated a bit and said, "When I say monitored, I mean in the presence of other staff members, until Taraji is comfortable in your presence. She needs to build up trust. We don't want to scare her, right?"

She paused to let her words sink in.

"You see," Mam' Dede continued, "unfortunately for Taraji, she is, as are many of our children, the result of crime in Soweto."

Mam' Candis came back, carrying stacked cups on a flat plate in one hand and a pot of hot water in the other. She put everything on top of one of the cardboard boxes and disappeared again. Then she came back with a cup filled with sugar and teaspoons.

Mam' Dede updated Mam' Candis on what she had said to Liva and Jacob as she poured steamy, reddish liquid into the cups.

"Have you ever tasted Rooibos tea?" asked Mam' Candis as she handed the cups to Liva and Jacob.

"This would be the first time," Liva admitted, taking the cup Mam' Candis offered.

"I've added some vanilla to bring out the natural sweetness; otherwise, it will taste earthy and like tobacco," Mam' Candis explained as they sipped the warm infusion.

"I wonder—" Liva hesitated. "I wonder why we never had direct contact with the orphanage."

They exchanged glances but didn't spot surprise on the faces of the two women. Jacob gave his wife an admonishing gaze.

"People almost always inquire on that," Mam' Dede assured Liva with a kind smile. "Most orphanages in Soweto are run with the aid of volunteers, you see? And the little money they have is to cover the essentials: food, beds, diapers, and so on. Our role in all this is to manage the paperwork." She studied the Danish couple. "Any other questions?"

"No, I was curious, that's all."

"Well," Mam' Dede smiled. "Are you ready?" she asked as she stood up.

"Three years ago," Liva said shakily.

Jacob passed one arm over Liva's shoulder and kissed her cheek, while nodding in silence.

The two ladies had them pass through the curtain, which led to a short hallway. It was even darker than the room they had just left. Down the hall, a room with long tables surely was the dining room. To the left, there was a door leading to the backyard. The noise of the playing children became clearer. It was a courtyard with lush mango trees. About twenty kids were playing.

"Taraji," called Mam' Candis.

A little girl in a pink T-shirt, blue shorts, and pigtails tied with matching pink ribbons turned to see who was calling.

Chapter

43

(2013)

"WHAT'S ON TV?" Mom asked me from the kitchen.

"*Family Trackers,* I think it's called. Come and sit here with me, so we can watch it together," I explained while making room on the couch for her.

"I'll join you when I'm finished in the kitchen."

"By the time you're done, you'll have missed half the program. Come and I'll give you a hand when it's over," I insisted.

"Okay," she replied.

Now she came, drying her hands with a tea towel resting on her shoulder.

"What is it about?" she asked, taking a seat.

"It's a guy from Vietnam who was adopted by Danish parents," I explained, without taking my eyes from the screen. "Now he wants to find his biological family. It's very interesting because the journalists have done research on his background, and they will travel to Vietnam to contact his family."

I turned to her and noticed that she was quite pale, as if she had been hypnotized.

"Mom! Is there something wrong? It's like you've seen a ghost."

We could hear Dad from the hallway, complaining that Carson could barely walk, as he went to the kitchen to fill a glass of water.

"What are my two princesses watching?" Dad asked, poking his red and sweaty head into the living room.

Mom rose from the couch, picked up a plate from the table and went straight to meet him.

It truly annoys me when she does that, I reflected. *For some mysterious reason, it's like she's lost in space and you have to take her arm to bring her back to reality. Then when you ask her what's wrong, she leaves without explanation and acts as if nothing has happened.*

I heard them whisper; mostly it was Mom's. When the TV show went on a commercial break, I jumped from the couch to join them in the kitchen.

When they saw me, both went silent.

"What's the hush-hush?"

"Nothing," said Dad, emotionless.

I saw Mom, who was still holding the dish she had brought from the living room. She turned to put it into the dishwasher.

"Sure," I said with a hint of irony.

I grabbed Carson, who was under the table, and went back to the living room to watch the rest of the program.

The chilling squeal of jammed brakes made us rush out of the house. We realized that something terrible had happened in the neighborhood and we could hear the howl of a wounded dog. When we reached the main road, there was no sign of any vehicle, only a lump of copper curls pulled to the side of the sidewalk.

I went to check if the freaking jerk had killed the dog, but I was happy to discover that the puppy was alive. I wasn't sure if I should touch it for fear of being bitten. However, the thought of leaving it there was not an option, so I pulled myself together and dared to touch its back.

"Why don't we wait for the owner?" Mom asked. "Someone must miss it, don't you think?"

Dad nodded.

"Why don't we take it home and if it survives the night, I'll put some posters up so they'll know whom to contact?" I proposed.

"What if Carson gets jealous?" Dad asked mischievously.

"Amusing. I'll take that as a yes," I said, while checking the tin plate on its collar.

It said: "Brandy." I took the dog in my arms. Except for the scratches on the forelegs, there was no indication of other injuries.

"Brandy stays with us until the owner appears," I announced, turning back to the house.

Chapter

44

"I'M COMING," I called on my way to the front door.

I yanked the door open to face the idiot who was pushing the bell button incessantly. "Jesus!"

"Hi!" the stranger said with a huge smile.

The vision of the guy standing in front of me took me by surprise. The phrase "beautiful boy" didn't do him any justice. I'd dare guess he was in his early twenties at most. His blue eyes framed by copper brown eyebrows made a charming contrast to his bleached hair. I blushed when he gave me a quizzical eye. Surely he noticed I was staring at his narrow torso.

"Yes?" I asked, trying to regain my composure.

He showed me a piece of paper. It was the "wanted" poster I had made to locate Brandy's owner.

"I'm Nicklas," he said, extending his hand.

"I'm Taraji, ahem, sorry for the way I opened the door ..."

"Never mind, I'm the one who should apologize. How's Brandy?"

I nodded. He must have been the owner, since I hadn't mentioned the dog's name on the posters.

"She' doing well. Dad took her to the vet to ensure there wasn't any internal bleeding. Brandy only had a few scratches on her front legs and a little shock, I guess. Follow me."

I waved him to the utility room.

When he came in, Brandy began to wag her tail, which confirmed he knew the dog. With a panther movement, Nicklas reached down and took Brandy in his arms. Brandy rested her head on Nicklas' shoulder.

I silently asked the sky to let me swap places with the puppy, if only for a few seconds. Suddenly, I became well aware of the old gray tee and worn-out sweats I was wearing and I wished I were somewhat more presentable.

"Please, I don't want you to believe we don't care about Brandy. But she has this thing for running away."

He scratched Brandy's back.

"You have nothing to explain. It took years to train Carson."

Hearing his name, Carson entered the utility room, dragging his back feet.

"A cocker spaniel." Nicklas laughed, perplexed.

"Yes, but Carson's old; he tires of walking from the kitchen to my bedroom," I told Nicklas as I crouched to scratch Carson's furry back.

"Carson?"

"If I got it right, he is a famous graphic designer. Mom's idol."

"How old is he?"

"I'm not sure because when Dad and Mom brought me here, Carson was just a puppy. I'm adopted from South Africa."

I was surprised to mention my adoption. Normally I didn't talk about that, unless someone asked directly. I guess something happened with Nicklas that I felt the urge to tell him.

His eyes lit up with a smile.

"From Cape Town?"

"Johannesburg, Soweto. Have you been to South Africa?"

"Haven't, but I've read a lot about Cape Town. I'd like to go, someday. What about you?"

"I've never been there, either, but I'd like to. I saw *Family Trackers* the other day. It was about a guy from Vietnam trying to find his family."

"I've seen it," he said, nodding. "Would you like to find your birth family?"

We heard footsteps in the hallway. It was Mom.

"Hello?" she greeted us inquisitively.

"Mom, this is Nicklas. Nicklas, Mom," I hurried to say.

She approached Nicklas to shake hands. She murmured her name as she studied him with an icy glare.

"You've done an excellent job with Brandy, thank you," Nicklas said, talking to both of us. "I would like to cover the vet expenses," Nicklas added, addressing Mom.

"No way Dad will accept that," I interrupted, dismissing the idea.

"I have to return the favor, don't you think?"

"You can visit us one of these days, if you want ..."

"Great idea." Nicklas smiled, showing a row of perfect white teeth. "Sure you guys don't want me to pay for the vet fees?"

"Sure."

Mom seemed perplexed but did not utter a word.

It was a fraction of a second, but long enough to feel a tickle in my stomach when I held his gaze just before heading to the front door.

"Nice meeting you, ma'am," he said, reaching out to shake Mom's hand.

Mom nodded and I followed him all the way to where my dad parked the old Volvo.

"What do you do? I've never seen you around here."

The question burst out of me and I felt pathetic, but Nicklas didn't seem to notice.

"I'm in my first year at CBS, Information Management, and I also do ten hours a week at 7-Eleven. And you?"

"Not much, I'm in my last year of high school. I run; I sometimes climb walls and take care of wounded dogs."

We laughed.

"Have you thought about what you're going to do next?"

"No idea, maybe take a gap year, travel a bit, volunteer in Soweto, and see what happens when I come back."

I heard Mom's voice from the house.

"Taraji."

I felt moisture on my hands and wiped them instinctively on my pants. When I raised my head, Nicklas was watching me with a serious expression.

"Your eyes."

"My eyes?" I asked, unsure I had heard right.

"Nothing," he said, cuddling Brandy in his arms and walking away slowly.

I felt a wave of heat crawling up my neck.

"I'm coming," I replied to my mom in an attempt to pull her back to reality.

A FAMILY LIKE THAT, Nicklas reflected on his way home, Brandy still in his arms. Immediately after, he dismissed the idea, ashamed of his lack of gratitude.

It was true that he never knew his dad, but Nicklas' mom gave him a home and stayed with him. Nicklas also learned all about bread.

His mom was a baker. She took over his grandparents' bakery in part because none of her sisters wanted the business, but the real reason was that she loved it. She loved the sweet smell of freshly baked bread coming out of the oven. She never resented leaving her bed at three in the morning to prepare the dough, wait for it to rise, and carefully put it in the oven. Another rule she never, ever broke was to rush the process of baking rye bread. "It takes the time it takes," was her motto.

The preparation of the bread was as important to her as the selection of the ingredients. More than once, Nicklas saw her dismiss a supplier who failed to deliver her preferred brand of flour.

The idea of expanding her business was remote, since it was unthinkable for her to industrialize the bread production. The only concession she made was when she bought the mixers, and that was only after she injured her right shoulder from hours of kneading the dough. It had almost forced her to find another job.

His mom's enthusiasm was contagious every time Nicklas saw her putting the paper doilies in the baskets for the apple bread, beer bread, scones, and muesli bread, like she was polishing crystal glasses; nothing should be out of place.

Funny coincidence. The dogs, her wish to visit South Africa ... He wondered what more they had in common.

"I HAVE AN idea I want to share with you," I announced.

Mom and Dad waited as I put a sausage on my plate, straight from the grill. There was mild moisture in the air, no wind, and we could hear the singing sparrows hiding under the leaves of the vine at the end of the terrace.

"Tell us," said Dad, holding a glass of beer.

"I'm going to write to *Family Trackers* to find out if they can help me find my family in Soweto."

About to take a bite of grilled chicken, Mom put the fork back on her plate and stared at me. Dad kept nodding blankly, his eyes wide open, and he finally met Mom's eyes for a second.

"W-why?" Mom stammered.

She took the jug of water and filled her glass halfway.

"Well ... I don't know. I guess I'm just curious. What do you think?" I wondered, now biting my index fingernail.

"Are you *going* to write? Or you wrote them already?" Mom asked, crossing her arms.

I hated that she was implying I had acted behind their backs. I took a deep breath.

"I wanted to talk to you first, but if you don't want me to, I'll drop it, okay?"

"Dear. It's not that ... I guess we are surprised you want to contact your family in South Africa, since you've never shown any interest, even though we've been very open ... Don't you think, Mom?" said Dad, trying to smooth over Mom's reaction.

But she didn't answer. Instead, Mom left the table to take care of the meat on the grill.

"Let's enjoy the meal and go together to the bonfire," Dad pleaded. "All I want is to have a nice St. John's Eve with my two princesses. Tomorrow would be a good day to talk all this through; what do you think?"

"No, Jacob, I don't think it's a good idea to showcase our private life in a ..." Mom paused, short of words; suddenly she recalled. "Reality show. Besides, we have no contact with the orphanage."

"Mom, you don't need to participate if you don't want to. As for the orphanage, don't worry. The program has a team of journalists for research and tracking. There's no guarantee they'll take my case. Do you know how many adopted people are in Denmark? I mustn't be the only—"

"We've told you all we know; why isn't that enough?" Mom interrupted.

"Mom, it was just an idea."

I dropped my arms, appalled at her reaction.

"Can we talk about this tomorrow?" Dad insisted.

Apart from the embers burning the meat on the grill, a heavy silence fell over us. A bumblebee fluttered near my glass filled with the remaining lemon soda. The scent of lilacs mixing with the smoke from the barbecue filled the air.

I couldn't figure out the reason why Mom was reacting like this. If I dared to share my plan, it was because they'd been so open about the adoption. I couldn't understand all the hush-hush around my birth parents. The worst part was Mom's silences. When something bothered her, she put me in the fridge for days. Meaning that in her world, I became some invisible matter, rather than her taking the trouble of telling me what the hell I did wrong.

I examined my plate. I picked at the sausage with my fork; the red liquid that flowed from it had now become an unappetizing, yellowish lard.

"Thanks for the food," I said quietly and went to the kitchen.

Mom said something I couldn't hear.

I crossed down the hall to my bedroom. Mom and Dad's were next to mine and there was a third door, which led to Mom's office. From there I could hear the noise of dishes and cutlery, so I gathered they were tidying up.

"Taraji, are you coming with us to the bonfire?" Dad asked as he entered in my bedroom.

"Pass."

I put the laptop aside, threw myself onto the bed, and covered my face with a pillow. I just didn't want to hear them leave.

"Are you sure you don't want to come? Some local celebrity will make a speech, and there will be hot cocoa … and beer, but not for you, young lady," said Dad, pulling my toes while speaking.

In a more serious tone, he added, "Taraji, your mom loves you. She only wants the best for you. Don't you forget that, okay?"

"Then why doesn't she want to help me?"

"If it's so important to you, we'll do everything we can to help you," said Mom from the door. "But I repeat, we do not have contact with the orphanage."

"Mom, I just want to know why she gave me up for adoption, that's all."

Mom came and hugged me; Dad wrapped us with his grizzly bear's hug.

"Taraji, don't judge her. It's not easy being a human being in Soweto," Mom dared to say, but Dad added, "Soweto and Farum are two different worlds, Taraji. Someday you'll understand. Are you sure you don't want to come to the bonfire with us?"

"No, I think I'd rather stay to finish my homework for tomorrow."

"If you decide to go out, remember to text, okay?" suggested Mom on her way out.

"Okay, Mom."

"LIVA, THERE WAS no need to lie to Taraji," Jacob admonished her. "You told her twice that we have no contact with the orphanage. Twice," he emphasized his words, forming a "V" with his fingers.

"So you' prefer that I tell her what they said at the orphanage?" she replied. "That's why Taraji always takes your side; you never stand by me."

"Wait a minute. That's not fair, Liva. We all knew this situation was coming; it's natural she wants to know where she comes from, and if she takes my side, it's only because I let her breathe."

"So I'm not a good mother?" Liva stopped to face Jacob.

"Hon, you are the best mother Taraji could ever have," he said, stroking her cheek gently.

Jacob paused to avoid the passers-by hearing their conversation.

"You know that, don't you? Just stop treating her like she's a little girl."

"Maybe you're right, thanks," Liva said, tongue-in-cheek.

"Maybe?"

They both burst out laughing.

Chapter

46

"MOM, MAY I use your computer to print out my presentation? It's very short, just four pages. I swear it won't take long ..."

I saw a faint cloud of steam rising through the open door of the bathroom when I poked my head in, as Mom was taking a shower.

"Sure, but hurry up," I heard her say from the shower.

Dad was making breakfast. I could smell the freshly brewed coffee in the kitchen. In the rush to print the document, I went barefoot down the hall and crossed diagonally to my mom's office.

Every time I entered her office, I had the sensation that this wasn't part of the house, maybe because the room was papered with a pattern simulating a log cabin. The L-shaped desk facing the back wall made it appear bigger. Two wide screens lay on the longer part of the "L" and a Mac computer sat on the shorter section. Facing the window was a white table for four people. The light wooden shutters gave the room a yellowish shade. The Mac was untouchable, since that was where Mom dealt with the heavy graphic stuff, so I chose the Dell.

I turned on the computer, and a series of green lights flickered on the router. After a couple of minutes, all the applications were ready for use. I took the flash drive I'd brought with me and inserted it into the USB port. I clicked on the PowerPoint icon and the hourglass appeared on-screen.

As I waited for the program to load, a series of blue windows began to emerge from the lower right corner of the screen. It was Outlook showing unread, incoming emails. There were many messages. There were two from Dad, one from some client, and if I saw correctly, one from Mercy May.

My heart began to pound violently and I pondered whether or not to read the Mercy May email. If I wasn't mistaken, Mercy May was the orphanage I heard Mom saying I came from.

We don't usually snoop around each other's stuff, and part of me was urging me to let it go. After all, Mom repeated that they had no contact with the orphanage, but still ... something fishy was going on here.

I just clicked on the "O" and the mail program opened after a few seconds. All emails were displayed on-screen. I tried to check the inbox, but the message list was so long and my heart was pumping so hard that I felt the throbbing in my tonsils. At any moment, Dad or Mom would stick his or her head in the office to remind me about breakfast.

I filled my lungs with air in a deep breath and checked again but found nothing. Suddenly, in the section on the right, I saw some folders that clearly suggested that Mom was filing messages according to the content. There was a folder that said "Delivered," the next said "Feedback," the one below that said "Pending," and the one following it said "Private." I opened the last folder and found a sea of emails and another subfolder that said "MM" in bold with a number one next to it, indicating the number of unread emails.

"MM" sounds like Mercy May, I thought.

Without thinking twice, I double-clicked on it and all the messages in the folder appeared. Lucky guess, since I confirmed that it was Mercy May. The first message was from the orphanage and thanked Mom and Dad for their last contribution.

I didn't have time to read all the messages, so I clicked on the first message and pressed Ctrl + A to select everything, Ctrl + C to make a copy of it, and finally Ctrl + V to paste it in the flash drive. A series of white envelopes appeared on-screen.

"Breakfast is ready," called Dad from the kitchen.

"One minute," I replied to keep him over there.

My heart almost stopped when I realized that I didn't have time to print the presentation, but now the important thing was to secure the emails. When the last envelope appeared, I closed the program and turned off the computer. I stood up and pushed the chair back in place. I turned to leave but jumped back in fright, instead.

Mom was watching me from the doorway, wearing a bathrobe and a towel wrapped around her head; a subtle whiff of verbena scent from the Marseille soap drifted in the air. Nothing seemed to indicate that she noticed.

"Mom, y-you scared me," I stammered.

"Oh, sorry, did you print your presentation?" she asked me, stepping into the room.

"I couldn't. I'll give it a try from the computer lab," I said, heading out of her office.

"Taraji."

"Aha?" I said without turning.

"You forgot your flash drive," she said, waving the device in her hand.

I retraced my steps to get the flash drive.

"Thanks, Mom," I muttered, unable to hold her gaze.

"You heard Dad. Breakfast is ready ..."

"Sure, I'm coming."

Chapter

47

LIVA

LIVA WENT TO the kitchen to make a cup of tea; she needed a break after so many hours sitting in front of the computer. Carson followed her, so she crouched down to give him a pat. She noticed that not much fur was left on his back as he went straight to sleep under the folding table.

It was nearly twelve but Liva was not hungry. It seemed that it had been only two hours since Jacob and Taraji had left the house.

The absence of noise was necessary and even pleasant, but only until 3 p.m. After that, the house became a huge black hole that sucked her in like a vacuum cleaner, and her desire to be together with Jacob and Taraji was almost unbearable.

She put some water in a kettle and busied herself washing the Thermos she'd brought from her office. She realized that she had missed the poster contest twice before, but not this year. This time, she was going to finish the designs with time enough to meet the due date. This was a personal project, something to feed her professional ego. You can call it what you wish, but no way was she going to miss it again.

Liva did care about the contest, but more profitable projects always stood in the way. Now it was different, as she did not want to lose the pulse of her artwork. Jacob did not understand much about these things when she tried to explain them to him. Not because he was materialistic, rather, maybe too pragmatic, but she guessed such contrasts kept them together.

The sound of the ringtone brought her back to earth. She recognized the tune she set for unknown calls. As she realized that her mobile was in the office, she ran down the hall and managed to answer on the fourth ring.

"Hello?"

"Am I speaking with Liva Ravn?" a man's voice inquired.

"Y-yes. Sorry, your name was ...?" she stammered.

"I'm calling you from the Furesoe police station. It's in connection with Taraji Ravn ..."

"What happened?" she asked as her vision darkened for a split second.

"We can call it a minor crime. So please come and pick her up. We will give you all the details in person."

"Minor crime? At least tell me, what did she do?"

Liva was appalled as she heard the man on the phone taking a deep breath.

"Shoplifting," he said impatiently.

"Excuse me? There must be an error ... Could I speak to her?"

"Actually, it would be better if you come. That's why we called you."

"May I talk to her?" she pushed.

"I'm afraid not, ma'am, you have to come in person."

"May I have the address?" she requested, giving up.

"At 24 Raadhustorvet Street, it's right across from Kumbelhaven garden."

"I'll be right there."

"Thanks."

She was perplexed for a few seconds as she recalled the boiling water for her tea. She went to the kitchen and turned off the stove.

Liva tried to reach Taraji on her mobile, but all she heard was "Three is a magic number" from the answering machine. After the third attempt, she decided to dial 25 25 25 25. A woman took the call almost immediately.

Liva told her that she needed a taxi, and the woman assured her that a car was on its way.

Liva waited in the kitchen, as if she was stuck in a cardboard box. Absently, she filled up Carson's water bowl and grabbed her jacket as she walked out the door. When she locked the door, the taxi was rolling slowly up her driveway.

"GOOD AFTERNOON, WHAT can I do for you?" said the police officer at the front desk.

"My name is Liva Ravn. I've come for Taraji Ravn."

"Sit down, please," he replied as he typed something on the keyboard of the computer in front of him. He pointed to a row of light wooden chairs lining both sides of the reception area.

As Liva sat down, she noticed a senior couple. They barely raised their heads.

The chairs matched the rest of the furniture and there was a round clock with Roman numerals on the wall. Another officer approached and motioned for her to follow him.

They went through one side of the desk and continued down the hallway with dark blue doors on both sides. The policeman stopped at the third door on the left and opened it to let Liva in. A tearful Taraji, wearing an angry expression, was sitting next to a female officer. From the fury in her eyes, Liva gathered that Taraji was far from happy to see her.

The agent closed the door and the woman sitting with Taraji updated Liva.

"This time, Taraji will only pay a fine, but the key issue here is to find out the root cause of this behavior and what to do in the future so it won't happen again," she said.

"Well, to put it mildly, I am so surprised that I don't know what to say." Liva licked her lips and continued, "Tara is not a troubled girl; she does pretty well at school. She is an active girl; what can I tell you?" Liva said as she tried to take her daughter's hand, but Taraji pulled away in disgust, which puzzled her.

"Taraji?" Liva asked but no response came from her daughter.

"You can go home now," the woman interrupted. "We will send the fine invoice by post in a couple of days."

Taraji walked to the exit in silence, head down.

They left the building and Liva hailed the first taxi they spotted and rode home without saying much. Even though Liva wanted to tell her daughter so many things, a mixture of surprise and rage froze all the words in her mouth. When the taxi parked in front of the house, Taraji almost jumped out of the car, ran inside the house, and locked herself in her room.

Chapter 48

LIVA

NOTHING IS THE same, Liva reflected, and the worse part was that she could not figure out what they did to infuriate Taraji like this.

Taraji spent the last two days locked up in her room and she only came out to go to the bathroom or to grab a snack from the fridge when Liva was not around.

Now it was Liva's turn "in the fridge," as Taraji would say when she upset her mother. Jacob was the only one who had the privilege to enter her room, but Taraji would not speak her mind with him, either.

Liva did not want to push her daughter; neither did she want to lose her. *It must be something about her biological parents*, Liva thought as she racked her brain to find out what was going on. She kept waking up at night bathed in sweat. Even in her dreams, Liva was haunted by the devastating threat of losing her forever.

Suddenly, Liva felt the urge to talk to Taraji, so she went straight to her room.

"Tara, I'd like to have a word with you." She knocked gently.

"Who is it?"

"Who else could it be? It's me, your mom," replied Liva, who heard Taraji pacing in her bedroom like a caged tiger.

"What?" she inquired after yanking the door open, one hand on her hip and the other holding the doorknob.

Liva realized that her Taraji had become another person. They had never spoken to each other this way. It pierced her heart to witness Taraji's behavior.

"We need to talk. This can't continue," Liva managed to say.

"About what?" Taraji challenged.

"Taraji, you owe us an explanation, today or tomorrow or in a year ..."

"There's nothing to explain," she said, biting the knuckle of her index finger.

"So you mean it is okay to steal?"

"So you mean it's okay to tell lies?" Taraji fired back.

"Lies? What do you mean?"

"This, this, and this!" she said, grabbing a bunch of papers from her desk. "Your lies."

She threw them at Liva, who saw the papers fall in slow motion, like flakes in snow globes.

Taraji stood still with crossed arms and smirked in triumph.

Her mother bent down to pick up the first sheet of paper she could reach; she felt the blood draining from her face as she read the email address of the orphanage.

"You said that you had no contact with Mercy May and now it turns out that you pay them every month," Taraji said in a scornful tone.

That hit Liva like a cement block. It was one thing that her own daughter caught her lying in a pathetic attempt to conceal the truth of her origins, but it was quite another thing that she seemed to question the reason for their contributions.

The sudden tide of rage did not come from her heart; otherwise, Liva would have felt the pain coming from her chest. This rage pumped right from her stomach, as if she pressed her belly and buttocks holding gas.

"BECAUSE THEY GAVE ME A DAUGHTER," Liva shouted.

Taraji jumped back. Her wide-open eyes and the slight tremor of her parted lips showed a great deal of fear.

Liva was also surprised by her own reaction. She guessed she just exploded after two days of enduring Taraji's indifference. On top of all that, Liva wondered if she really had to take her own daughter's veiled remarks.

Taraji bit her index fingernail. Again! She did it whenever she was nervous and sometimes Liva wondered if there was any nail left to bite.

"That orphanage gave me a daughter and I'm going to be indebted to them for the rest of my life," Liva whispered, afraid of scaring her even more. "All the money in the world can't compensate for the joy those people brought to this house."

Exhausted, Liva sat on the edge of Taraji's bed and covered her face.

Taraji stood motionless, almost nailed to the floor. Her rust-colored eyes seemed as if they would jump out of their sockets at any time. It was the first time Liva had ever yelled at her.

"Yes, I lied, and I might have lost your trust. At night, I feel like I'm drowning, but I also know I couldn't have handled this situation differently."

"Mom, som—" Liva heard Taraji say.

"Taraji, you want the truth? Okay. You are entitled to know the truth," she insisted, now the tears rolling down her eyes.

"Mom, Mom, the door ..."

"No, no, it's okay, let me finish, Taraji," Liva said, lowering her head. "All we know is that your mom was a teenager; she went out to buy something, the assault, the pregnancy. That's all we know," Liva confessed, her eyes glued to the floor. She was sobbing so hard that she could barely talk. Then when she raised her head, Taraji was gone.

Liva ran out of the bedroom as her daughter was heading to the front door. When she reached Taraji, she opened the door.

Brandy's owner was standing there, boasting a smile worthy of a TV commercial.

This was what Taraji had been trying to tell her back in her bedroom, Liva realized as she went back to the hallway, since she didn't want Nicklas to see her crying.

"Hi Nicklas, nice to see ya," said Taraji, smiling.

Taraji stared at her mother as she grabbed the dog from Nicklas' arms. Liva suddenly realized that she had not seen Taraji's dimples for quite a long time

"Is this a good time?" he asked, sensing a sort of tension between the two of them.

"It couldn't have been better. How's Brandy doing?" Taraji asked, glancing at Liva over her shoulder.

"Well, Brandy is fully recovered. I came 'cos you said we could pop by, but if it isn't a good time ..."

Liva thought Tara was going to send him away. Instead, she pulled him into the house.

"I'll be in my office," Liva muttered, not knowing what to do with herself.

Chapter

49

NICKLAS' VISIT COULDN'T have been more timely. I shook the thought and tried to focus on Nicklas and Brandy.

"Want something to drink?"

"Like what?"

"Don't know—water, tea, soda?"

"Soda."

"Come and tell me what you've been doing."

I beckoned him on my way to the kitchen.

We entered and Carson was still lying under the folding table. He lifted his head to greet the visitors, wagged his tail, and settled back down.

"Don't know if there's any fizz left; we bought it for the grill on Midsummer's Eve. Try it."

Nicklas put Brandy on the floor and grabbed the glass I gave him. He took a short sip.

"All right," he said.

He took a longer sip, a little pause, two more sips, and there was nothing left in the glass.

"Want more?" I asked, still holding the plastic bottle.

He handed me the glass and nodded.

While I was refilling, I caught him checking me out.

"Are you okay?" he asked

"I'm fine. Do you run?" I asked, pointing at his jogging pants in an attempt to change the conversation to a more neutral subject.

"I've been running the last three years."

I smiled.

"Where?"

"Where, what?"

"I mean, where do you usually run?"

"Ah, yes! Well, it depends. Sometimes, I take the road from where I live to the park and back to Kumbelhaven. That's about three miles. You must know the park. It's near Farum Bytorv."

Kumbelhaven, did he know? I thought. That's pretty close to the police station and I wondered if he knew. This was too much of a coincidence. I observed him to find a hint but I couldn't tell.

"What? Did I say something wrong?"

"No, no. Is that the only jogging spot you run?"

"No, I also run in Copenhagen around the lakes, in Faelledparken too, and when Mom lends me the car, I drive to Utterslevmosen. I like to change the route to stay motivated. What about you? Have you ever run?"

"Yes, but never out of town."

"If you want to, we can try Utterslevmosen. It's not that far; I can borrow Mom's car so it won't take long."

"You mean today?"

"Why not?"

"I don't know ..." I said, scratching my head.

Suddenly I realized it wasn't a bad idea after all; that way I could avoid Mom until Dad came back.

"I warn you; I'm not a fast runner."

"Not gonna leave you behind."

"Okay. I'll tell Mom."

I stuck my head in Mom's office and saw her sitting in front of the Mac, immersed in some poster design.

"Mom, Nicklas invited me to run in Utterslevmosen," I announced.

"Utterslevmosen?" Mom asked as she checked her watch. "Are you taking the bus?"

"No, we will take his mom's car; we have to stop by his place to leave Brandy, anyway."

"How old is Nicklas? I thought he was your age."

"Old enough to have a driver's license," I replied and regretted it came out harsher than intended.

"I'll talk to him," said Mom, now turning in the direction of the kitchen.

"Please, Mom, don't embarrass me; I promise I'll leave the car if he drives like crazy," I begged.

"If he drives like crazy, you get out of that car, and call me immediately. I'll pick you up, okay? Promise me."

"Promise."

I ran to my bedroom to change clothes.

"Don't forget a bottle of water and a jacket," Mom called from her office.

"I won't."

It was pretty easy to find what to wear. I took the only running outfit I had: the ancient black running tights, the black and grey running crewneck—now pale grey after so many washes—no-show running socks, and an old pair of Asics.

I was about to give up on the running jacket when I recalled it was hanging behind the door together with my black running cap.

"See you," I called from the hallway.

Nicklas was in the utility room, playing with Brandy and Carson. On our way out, I filled two plastic bottles with water and took two bananas from the fruit bowl.

"Let's go."

Chapter 50

"MOM GOT NERVOUS when I told her you'd drive," I said as we were heading to Utterslevmosen.

"Really? There's nothing to be afraid of; I'm Mr. Careful."

It was almost 3 p.m. when we took the exit toward Hareskovej and the traffic slowed. I guessed all the people who worked in Copenhagen were now driving back home.

"And you think I'm a bad driver?"

"How could I know?" I admitted with a shrug. "But if you brake suddenly or if you crash into a tree, I think I'll notice," I said as I pulled some skin from the base of my nail.

"How old are you?"

"Take a guess," Nicklas challenged me.

"Nineteen, tops."

"Twenty-one," he said, without taking his eyes off the traffic. "And you?"

"Sixteen. Well, almost seventeen."

"Almost there," he said, pointing with his left thumb as he stopped the car at the traffic lights. We turned toward Mosesvinget. I was surprised that it wasn't a park but the main route of a residential area.

"I thought we were going to the park," I said.

"Come on, don't be disappointed. This is a residential area, but there is a lake and geese and ducks and sheep, and people run."

"Don't get me wrong; I just expected a park. This place is filled with houses, that's all."

He smiled back and I kept staring out of the window. The houses were amazing and I could see people running down a gravel path on the left.

The path narrowed as we ended on Engsvinget Street. We turned to the left. Then Nicklas reversed slowly to park the car by the sidewalk.

Outside the car, the wind blew the scent of green apples from one of the houses where they had just mowed the lawn. We walked past the intersection of Mosesvinget and Engsvinget Streets. Nicklas stopped.

"Normally I take two loops of about 3.1 miles each, but we can do a short run of 1.8 miles if you want."

"Let's keep it short ..." I suggested.

"Okay, let's find out how much time it takes us at your pace," he said while touching his training watch, and I realized it was a Garmin Forerunner 405.

"What a piece of gear you've got!" I exclaimed. "Are you happy with it?"

"Yes, I am, but I don't use all the features."

"Everyone says this is so sophisticated that you almost need to do a course to use it. Is it true?"

When I raised my head his eyes fixed on me. He blushed.

"Let's run. It's getting late and I don't want your mom bitchin' at me."

"I don't care if she's angry," I said. "Where do we start?"

"See the speed sign over there?"

"Aha."

"When we reach the sign, we'll warm up for about five minutes, so we start to run, okay? Are you ready?"

"Sure."

We jogged slowly; 50 yards to the right, there was a clear spot with benches and picnic tables. The geese took over a football field to the left. We stopped to let a mother duck and her ducklings cross the street and resumed along the path until we reached a spot lined with willows.

"What do you think now?" Nicklas asked, as his face was turning sweaty and red.

"Love it."

"Ready to run?"

"Yes."

We ran at a casual speed. Nicklas was about three steps ahead of me and occasionally turned his head to make sure I was right behind him. We passed the line of lush willows, which resembled a tunnel, and at the end there was a house with a thatched roof.

"After that house we'll end up on Groennemose Alle Street," he said.

As we passed the house I grew slightly disappointed, as from that point, there was no gravel nor lake. It was only a half-mile track in both directions. Nicklas ran to a clean spot leading to the lake. The sunlight reflecting on the water was like crumpled aluminum foil. Thousands of ducks, doves, and herons fluttered in all directions. I slowed down a little to enjoy the scenery; Nicklas ran past me, tapping his watch to remind me of the time.

"There's not much left," I heard him say.

"Sure?" I managed to ask.

"Yes."

He was red, sweaty, and judging by the smile on his face, also happy.

In the end, we ran to the left again to close the loop we had begun between Mosesvinget and Engsvinget Streets. We reached the patch of land that showed another side of the lake. Here the grass was tall and dry. The main road wasn't far.

Nicklas was right; there isn't much farther distance to the car, I thought.

Nicklas sprinted the rest of the distance to the car. I tried not to be intimidated by his speed, so I ran as fast as I could. When I reached the car, my whole skin throbbed and I had a metallic taste in my mouth.

"Well done, girl. 1.8 miles in 17:02 minutes," he announced.

"Nice to hear," I said between gasps. "Actually, I don't know if it's good or bad. When I run alone, I just walk if I'm tired. This is the first time I've run the whole distance without stopping. What are you laughing at?"

"You put it like you just ran a marathon. 1.8 miles is nothing."

"Well, not a big deal for you," I nudged him gently. "Feel like having a banana? I brought water too."

"Sure."

I grabbed the bag I brought with me and rummaged in it. I could feel that one of the bananas was all smashed. I gave him the good one and took what I could eat of the other one.

"We could have shared this one," said Nicklas.

I dismissed the idea with a smile.

"Next time, we'll climb walls in Humlebaek," I warned him with a smile.

"Any special gear?"

"We rent all that at the gym. If you like it, you can buy your own stuff."

"Deal," said Nicklas. Then he asked, "You're mad at your mom?"

The question gave me the sensation of traveling at high speed through a subway tunnel, as the wave of feelings I had been suppressing since Mom told me what happened in Soweto overflowed in a crying fit.

I cried like a spoiled child until hiccups made me bend forward. Nicklas moved closer and tried to hug me, but a side stitch kept me curled up. He opened the car door and I sort of slumped in the passenger seat.

Through the windshield, I saw him move over to the driver's seat, like he was running away from a rainstorm. This time he didn't utter a single word. I wept with my face hidden in my hands. Nicklas put his hand on my hand. I did not know how long we stayed like that.

At one point, Nicklas put the key in the ignition, careful not to make any noise so as not to break the silence.

When we returned home, he drove slowly into the driveway. We glanced at each other for a while.

"I'm here if you want to talk," he offered.

"Thank you, Nicklas. May I call you Nick?"

"You bet."

This time, his smile grew broader and his lovely teeth gleamed like pearls.

Uh oh, I'm getting fond of this smile, I thought.
I smiled back at him and walked slowly toward the house.

Chapter

51

WHEN I OPENED the door, a vanilla scent enveloped me. I closed my eyes and took a deep breath. Mom would still recount to anyone who wanted to hear that when they brought me home from Soweto, I had trouble eating. She would go on, telling them how hard it was for her and Dad to find something I liked. One day, Dad made pancakes stuffed with vanilla ice cream and strawberry jam. The killing touch was the sprinkle of icing sugar Dad gave them before serving.

Since then, they realized that there was no problem with my jaws. If I didn't want to eat, Dad would come with the baked pancakes, and I could eat them all.

For me, Dad's pancakes were the best. No one made them so thin and folded them as neatly on the tray as he did before putting them in the oven.

I realized that it had been ages since the last time we enjoyed them. I suspect it was my fault because I was watching my weight. I was as skinny as a needle, but nothing terrified me more than losing control of my shape and not looking like Naomi, my idol fashion model.

I went straight to the kitchen.

"We were worried; why didn't you call?" Mom admonished me.

"I forgot," I said and gave Dad a kiss on the cheek.

"It didn't occur to you that we were truly concerned?"

"I told you; I lost track of the time."

"Okay, okay, okay, who wants to eat?" said Dad, giving Mom a warning look.

"I'll help with the table," I told them on my way to the cabinet to pick up the plates.

I think I'm so mad at Mom because she lied, I thought, but I must admit that I was touched when she said she paid the orphanage because she had a daughter. I didn't dare to stare at her and say thank you for all that she'd done for me. I thought of the emails I found. If Mom had nothing to hide, what was so wrong with meeting my biological mother then?

"Taraji?" insisted Dad

"Yeah?" I said, shaking my head.

"I guess it's this Nicklas, isn't it?" Dad asked with a grin. "We need silverware."

"It isn't Nick, all right?" I said, faking annoyance.

"Ohh, sorry. Now you call him Nick ..." he nudged me teasingly. "When will I meet him?"

"I guess one day you're here when he comes."

AT HOME, MOM was the reason, the sense, and the rule. She was in charge of the bank accounts, as well as of paying the bills. She attended the meetings at my school. She made sure that my clothes matched the season and kept an eye on me so I did my homework.

I remember it was Mom who took me on Saturdays to the library to hunt for books written by Astrid Lindgren, A.A. Milne, and my favorite, Roald Dahl. She also took me to the Children's House at the Louisiana Museum to daub myself with paints or just to walk around the lake.

Mom studied my friends and at a stroke the verdict fell: "Simone is not a good influence for you, my dear." Unfortunately, she was right, but I would not admit it.

"Here are some beans, so you can dance all night long without stopping," Simone had said, as she tucked a little plastic bag into my pocket. There were two pastel-colored pills with the word *SKY* engraved on them. This was long before the shoplifting thing. Going to the Shopping Center in Farum was also Simone's idea. We entered Cassandra Noir, filled with confidence, to check out the latest fashions in lingerie. My blood ran cold when I saw her shoving hipsters and bras into her

Louis Vuitton canvas bag. She confessed that the bag was a counterfeit she had bought in Thailand the previous summer. Her fearlessness gave me goose bumps. She didn't even mind that I was standing there. When one of the saleswomen noticed, she called a security guard.

It never occurred to me to leave her alone. The shop manager decided to press charges, so they called the police. Simone was registered for shoplifting and I was reported as her accomplice. That was how I ended up at the police station in the first place. When I think of it, that lady at the lingerie shop deserved it. She always stared at me with such scorn, like she had to keep an eye on me, like every single black person in this world was a thief. And it wasn't even me who looted the stuff but the white and sophisticated Simone.

Dad, in contrast to Mom, was the negotiator, the moderator.

When Mom and I were mad at each other, he made a nice meal, where he would make us sit down and discuss our differences. Dad was the traditions keeper. He encouraged us to buy a Christmas tree in November. "December flies," he would say. He remembered everyone's birthdays, Morten's Goose in November, the cream buns in February, the bonfire for Midsummer's Eve. He neither missed the almonds in the *ris a la mande* on Christmas Eve nor the fireworks for New Year's Eve.

My first bike came in a giant cardboard box with Dad in it, disguised as Santa Claus. I could tell, because tangled in the handle was Santa's beard, revealing his round face, translucent with sweat and a smirk of satisfaction for the accomplished mission.

These pancakes were his way of saying we needed to talk.

APART FROM THE barely audible hiss of flickering candles placed on the table, we ate the pancakes in silence, and when we finished, Dad put the dishes aside.

"Taraji, we would like to address some issues," he sternly announced.

Mom was about to say something, but Dad put his hand on her lap to let him finish. Mom sighed and leaned back on her chair.

I plaited my fingers to hide their slight tremor, but I couldn't prevent my heart from pounding faster, awaiting the confrontation.

"We want to apologize," he said quietly.

"Huh?" I asked, unsure I had heard right.

I was reported for shoplifting at the police station. I had to pay a fine. I hadn't talked to Mom for the last few days and here he was, asking for forgiveness. A mixture of guilt and shame fell over my shoulders with the weight of a bag of cement.

"Yes, Taraji, we are very sorry because we have hidden things, things you have a right to know. We told you half-truths when you were old enough to understand. We are sorry that we still treat you like the little girl we brought home from Soweto."

He took a deep breath.

"If you want to meet your family, we are willing to take you there," Dad said, lowering his head and continuing hoarsely. "We had two contacts at Mercy May: Mam' Dede and Mam' Candis. Unfortunately, a couple of years ago, Mam' Dede died of diabetes, leaving Mam' Candis in charge."

Now it was Dad who wove his fingers together.

"Regarding the payments you saw in the emails, we have nothing to be ashamed of. Thanks to that orphanage, you are here with us, and we will continue to contribute indefinitely, so that other children will also have the same opportunity that you had."

Dad emphasized each word by tapping the table with his index finger, as he heaved a deep sigh and watched me.

"We need to know what you want to do," Mom added.

"I don't know," I said, shaking my head, unable to meet their eyes.

Chapter

52

"TARAJI!"

I stopped and rolled my eyes without turning. *Please, not him again*, I thought.

I was almost sure it was Mr. Boch. Mom told him everything about the shoplifting thing with the intention of rooting out Simone's influence on me, and now the man had become my shadow. During breaks, he didn't lose sight of me for a single second. I turned to find out what he wanted. My heart skipped a beat. It wasn't Mr. Boch but Nicklas, and it felt like ages since the last time I'd seen him.

"Nick?" I couldn't believe my eyes. "So nice to see you; where have you been? It's been ages since the last time, about a month ago?"

"Yeah, more or less," he said, lowering his head. "One: a nasty assignment on the Fundamentals of Reporting of Information Systems, two: the shifts in 7-Eleven, and three: I don't have your phone number, so I decided to try my luck here. Came yesterday, but I didn't find you."

"Yesterday it would have been impossible to find me here; we were all on an offsite day. A guided visit to the Black Diamond. Have you been there?"

"You mean the new building at the Royal Library? Never been there. You like it?"

"Yeah, I mean it was interesting, but the best of it all was the Segway ride at the end of the day. We had so much fun," I said, smiling. "How's Brandy?"

"Mom says she is biting everything within reach."

"How's that?"

"I moved to Copenhagen to be closer to CBS."

My smile became a grin that gave me the sensation of wearing a mask.

"I guess we will not be able to hang out as we used to ..."

I focused on a stone on the ground to avoid his gaze.

"Wondered if you want to come with me to the Coldplay concert at Parken Stadium tomorrow?"

"Really? Tomorrow is Tuesday."

"There was this contest at CBS, I was one of the three winners, what do you say?"

"I'd love to, but I have to ask permission."

"Fair enough," he said. "Want me to take you home?"

"Yeah, but before going any further, give me your phone number," I said as I rummaged in my bag to fish out my mobile.

Nicklas laughed and took his cell phone out of his pocket.

IT TOOK ME a little over two hours to tame my curls, but I was happy with what I saw in the mirror. I applied a light coat of copper color to my lips to emphasize my natural tan. I was wearing a gray, long-sleeved flannel shirt, slightly flared jeans, and black velvet heels.

"You look gorgeous," Mom praised me from the doorway.

Then her eyes fell on my high heels.

"Are those practical for a concert?" she added with a half-smile, knowing the answer.

"I've brought these, in case I get tired," I said while rummaging in my bag for the pair of flats I had tied with a red elastic band.

When I took them from my bag, a pile of folded papers fell to the floor.

"Nicklas is here," we heard Dad calling from the hallway.

"I'm going to say hello," Mom said.

"Would you please tell him that I'm almost ready?"

"Sure," Mom said on her way to the kitchen.

I pulled my black leather jacket from the closet, then I tried to pick up the clutter of old papers that sprang from my bag. I shook my head at the amount of old rubbish: a half-pack of Mentos mints, tickets for the movie *Picture This*, paper tissues, and old receipts from the snack bar in high school. Since I didn't have time, I sort of piled them up on the nightstand so I could remember to throw them away when I came back. Then a plastic bag with two colorful pills fell through the papers. Simone's beans and her mischievous smile came to mind. I studied the bag for a while and put it in my pocket.

"Why not?" I whispered.

"Why not what?" asked Mom, standing by the door.

I jumped and turned around. I should have gotten used to Mom walking around the house like a ninja.

"Mom, you scared me. I was considering bringing these mints," I said, showing her the candies.

"One thing, Taraji."

Uh oh, I thought. *This is serious. Every time Mom says, "one thing."*

"Be careful, all right? Don't drink from a bottle you haven't opened yourself."

"Sure."

"Something else, we can pick you up, in case Nicklas can't take you home, okay?"

"Mom, promise you're not going to show up over there."

She nodded with some reluctance.

"Okay," she muttered.

I took the jacket lying on the bed and Mom hugged me.

"Have fun, Taraji."

I hugged her back as quickly as I could and hurried down the hall to meet Nicklas, who was in the living room chatting animatedly with Dad.

"Nicklas was telling me about the subjects he's dealing with at CBS."

My eyes were on him; he was wearing blue jeans, a chalk-white flannel shirt, and a black leather jacket. His fringe was slicked back with hair gel. A subtle lemon scent reminiscent of CK One emanated from him, but I wasn't sure.

"Er," said Dad, "you guys better hit the road."

Mom looked at Dad and repeated, "hit the road?"—surprised by his way of talking.

We all laughed.

"But the concert is at 9:30 p.m.," Mom said.

"That's right, ma'am," said Nicklas, "but we need to get there early to find a parking spot."

"Parken Stadium must be crowded," Dad said, hugging Mom like a grizzly bear. "We're getting old." Nicklas gazed at me without saying a word. By the sparkle in his eyes, I would dare to say that there was a flash of admiration. My stomach tickled.

Chapter

53

WE ARRIVED AT the concert at 8:30 p.m. We drove around with the hope of finding a place to park. Unfortunately, even though we were early, the only option seemed to be to drive out of the concert area, but the side streets were jammed with cars. We ventured onto Jagtvej Street, which was also crammed. The miracle happened on Sankt Kjelds Gade Street. Nicklas parked his little Fiat parallel to the wall of the church and we laughed at the distance we had to retrace. I checked my heels and pulled the flats from my bag.

"Well done," Nicklas said, opening the door for me.

"Is it okay if I leave these heels in the car?"

"Of course," he assured me, reaching out to take my hand.

Nicklas almost dragged me through Noerre Allé. I thought we were going to cross Faelledparken, but Nicklas didn't think it was a good idea since it was getting dark. The route he chose ended up being the shortest.

Packed with long lines of people at the entrance, the queues were moving fast. Nicklas' eyes scanned all directions, I guess to take the atmosphere in. As we waited our turn to walk in, I heard a series of beeps on my cell phone. It was a text message from Mom.

Have a great evening my dear, kisses Mom, Dad & Carson.

I showed it to Nicklas.

"I, too, hope you like it," he said, lowering his head, almost as if he was afraid that this wasn't good enough for me.

"Sure, I'm very grateful," I said, as I gave him a kiss on the cheek.

He seemed surprised and took my hand as we looked around. There was tremendous energy. It was like we were about to watch a UEFA final football match.

When Nick showed the tickets at the entrance, the ushers showed us the neon bracelets we had to wear during the concert. They were pink, blue, yellow, and green. Nicklas picked the green and I preferred the pink one.

Once we were inside Parken, the stadium felt ready to burst and I realized that in the rush, I didn't visit the toilet before leaving home. I mentioned it to Nick and he agreed to escort me to the toilets. We stood in line again but it didn't take that long. My turn came, I entered, washed my hands when I finished, but there was no paper to dry my hands. I reached into my bag for the tissues in the little pocket. Then I remembered the "beans." Without thinking, I swallowed them and took a sip of water from the faucet.

Simone, this time it's me who'll have something to talk about, I thought with a smile, as I wiped my hands on my pants and left.

The concert was about to begin. Miraculously, Nick and I made our way close to the stage. The security crew had put a fence about six feet from the stage, which formed a corridor where Chris Martin and the rest of the band could move. At the back of the stage were two large screens, and on either side were towers holding the speakers that would carry the sound to every corner of the stadium.

When we made it to the fence, "Mylo Xyloto" was almost over, when a hint of "Hurts Like Heaven" began and a shower of confetti shaped like hearts and butterflies and trees fell from above, covering us. The sky turned pink and the thunder of applause filled the stadium. From where we were standing, we could see the piano sprayed with drawings similar to those in the tunnels leading to the train station. I hugged Nick as I planted a kiss on the corner of his lips.

I caught a glimpse of astonishment in his eyes.

I guess I got carried away by the music and felt the urge to dance and jump. Things slowed down when Chris Martin sang "In My Place." Although we were in the open, the heat was suffocating. I took off my jacket and stuffed it in my bag as best as I could.

"Are you that hot?" Nicklas asked in disbelief. I danced on, but this time with "Princes of China" sounding in the background. The concert was at its peak and I felt like I was the supreme queen of the universe, although my mouth was dry and the heat was unbearable.

Suddenly, the music ceased to blow in my ears and thousands of twinkling, moving lights resembled the climbing pythons of the club in Humlebaek. The towers holding the speakers made a fantastic climbing wall. An inner voice gave me an order to escape. I felt the heat like a chicken in the oven. The only way out was climbing the tower.

I thought I heard Nick saying something about going to the toilets and he made me promise not to leave this spot. I nodded.

Nicklas disappeared in the tumult and I moved to the left, closer to the base of the tower. I spotted the security crew. They all wore blue flannel shirts with white lettering on their chest and backs. They stood there, staring blankly, totally absorbed by the multitude of hysterical girls screaming, like me, just two feet away.

I eased forward as far as I could and grasped the base of the tower. One of my flats disappeared into a black bag of what seemed like rolled wires, so I took off the other shoe and began to climb.

It was easy and liberating. I just had to climb to escape the heat. Some people began to point at me, yet their attention went back to the stage where an elated Chris Martin, whose face was just inches away from the piano keys, was introducing "Viva la Vida." Now fifty thousand voices became one in a deep "ohohohohoh-ooooh- ohohohohoh."

I continued my way to the top of the tower and the night breeze gave me chills. My shirt was soaked and it clung to my arms. From that point, I saw several men at the base of the tower trying to climb up and thousands of green, pink, and white lightning bugs waving slowly from the left to the right.

The crowd is calling you, Taraji, said an inner voice. *Yes! Taraji, the crowd's calling ...*

The music stopped suddenly, as if someone had pulled the plug from the microphones. *The pack below will carry you. Don't be afraid, just jump, jump*, said the voice, sometimes chanting, sometimes whispering.

I took a deep breath, closed my eyes, and jumped.

Chapter

54

NICKLAS

"AREN'T YOU TAKING the phone call?" Nicklas' mom asked him when she saw him pocketing the smart phone after checking who was calling.

Nicklas shook his head in response.

"You look sad," she said as she stroked her son's hair.

"C'mon, I'm not a kid anymore," he said, trying to dodge her hand.

"Son, I'm just concerned; you seem sad. Something to do with Taraji?"

He tried to lead the conversation toward how things were going in the bakery and how Brandy was doing, but his mom kept turning the topic back to Taraji.

Nicklas was not sure he wanted to tell his mom that after leaving the hospital that night when Taraji did her crowd surfing, he never went back or kept in touch. But Taraji was determined to bombard him with text messages and phone calls.

"Nicklas, what happened with Taraji?" she insisted.

"Nothing, she's just very spoiled, that's all …"

"How spoiled?" his mom pressed.

Nicklas gave up. He knew she would insist until he gave her the whole shebang, so he told her.

"I took her to a concert and she jumped from a tower in the middle of the concert. The worst part was that it was *me* who had to call Liva and Jacob to give them the bad news."

He felt again the uneasiness building in the pit of his stomach. He guessed it was a mixture of repressed sadness and disappointment at what happened that night.

"I stayed at the hospital until Liva and Jacob arrived," he continued, unable to look his mom in the eye. "Then the doctors gave us the news that Taraji was under the influence of drugs. I think that they believed it was my fault." Nicklas shook his head in disapproval.

"Was it?"

"Of course not," he snapped.

"Are they mad at you?"

"I knew nothing about that. I told them I don't do drugs; you should know that," Nicklas said without looking up.

As they remained in silence, Nicklas snatched the opportunity. "Mom, why did you never marry again?" he asked.

She smiled and said, "I thought we were talking about you ..."

Nicklas had surprised her with the question, since his mom always had an answer at hand. She grabbed her mug with both hands, took a sip of coffee, and looked through the window.

"Why do you want to know?"

"I've always wondered why you never had a boyfriend ..."

"The bakery doesn't give much time to go out looking for a boyfriend. You were very little back then, and I don't know, I guess the opportunity never presented itself. Do you miss having a father figure?" she asked, as her cheeks sort of drooped in a sad expression.

"Yeah, maybe," Nicklas replied, scratching his head. "I don't want to make you sad. It's just that sometimes I wonder why I don't have a dad like the rest of my classmates, but it also worries me that you're alone, now that I have moved out."

"Nicklas, I'm alone, but I'm not lonely," she replied, shaking something from her sleeve.

"Don't you need the company of a man?"

"Yes, of course I do, but men are only good at quickies."

Nicklas looked up, surprised to hear her speaking like that.

"Of course! Except you, son," she hurried to say when she saw the hurt expression on his face. "I'm talking about your father and the way he disappeared when he found out I was pregnant."

"Bitter?" he asked, while taking Brandy in his arms.

"Word of honor," she said, one hand holding the mug and the other over her chest, like she was taking an oath to the queen. "I can live with the fact that your dad didn't want me. My problem is that he didn't show any interest in you. That, I can't forgive.

"As for another boyfriend, when I was little, your grandpa passed away and your granny went desperate so another man moved in shortly after. He made me press his shirts and if they weren't perfect, I had to start all over. He also wanted me to call him Dad and your granny never stood by me. I didn't want you to take orders from a stranger. I wanted you to be safe and happy, so I don't regret anything," she said, putting the mug on the table.

"You did good, Mom," Nicklas said, taking her hand.

"Returning to the subject, don't you think it's time to make peace?" she asked.

They both laughed.

Chapter

55

ACCORDING TO THE doctors, I fell about twenty feet, broke my right leg, left hip, elbow, and two ribs, but there was no damage to my spine. It seemed that I landed in a kneeling sort of position on a bag filled with wires, which helped cushion the fall.

Those twenty-seven days in the hospital gave me a few lessons about whom I could count on. My schoolmates sent flowers, a poem, and even recorded a video message by cell phone. I laughed as much as I could without hurting myself.

Simone never called. She must have been busy shoplifting or giving out beans. I didn't blame her. What happened at the concert was my decision and my responsibility. Nobody pushed me, just as no one pressed me to stick with her at the shopping mall.

Nicklas never showed up at the hospital and I didn't blame him, either. He must have been truly mad at me for what I'd done. That was the price I had to pay for taking him for granted; I missed him badly.

I started using crutches, but I'd still need a wheelchair to avoid overloading the other leg.

I heard footsteps coming down the hall. In this wing of the hospital, there wasn't as much activity as in the trauma section.

Dr. Knudsen and Mom opened the door, followed by Dad.

"How are you?" Dr. Knudsen asked with a smile.

He instinctively pushed up his glasses, as if they were about to fall from his nose. I noticed the fat fingers and spotless nails. The doctor was tall and his baritone voice filled the room.

"I'm ready to go home if you allow it ..."

"Yes, as far as I'm concerned, you're ready to go, but you have to start with caution and most importantly, you have to continue the rehab."

He paused.

"You were lucky this time; I guess your age could be a factor. The faster you stand up from that wheelchair, the better."

He looked at both Dad and Mom.

"See you in three weeks and remember to set an appointment before you leave."

Dr. Knudsen shook hands with Mom and Dad, then headed to the door.

"Stay away from ecstasy. You are better than that, okay?" he said over his shoulder.

I blushed with shame and looked down as he left. I hit rock-bottom in many ways when I fell from the tower. It was time to climb up and straighten things. I guessed that was what people called "coming of age."

"I'm sorry. I'm so sorry," I told my parents, lowering my head as I could no longer repress the tears. I was tired of playing hard, I-don't-give-a-damn-ass.

Mom and Dad rushed to hug me. "We're not mad at you, young girl. We were wild, too, at your age and made lots of mistakes," he said gently.

"Your dad's right, Taraji. How can we be mad at you? We love you," Mom added as she stroked my hair. "Let's just put this behind us. Let's get out of here; what do you think?"

We agreed. Mom offered to push the wheelchair to the exit. Dad took the bag with my stuff and held the door to let us out of the room. In that brief moment when Mom led me from the room into the hallway, I realized that they had aged. Dad's carefree smile was gone and the shadows under his eyes betrayed the sleepless nights.

Mom's clothes hung loosely on her frame; I guess she lost some weight this past month. Her hair was greasy and slight cracks ran down from both sides of her mouth.

It's my fault; I did this to them, I thought with deep regret.

Down the hall, we stopped at the nurses' station to make my next appointment. Mom approached the nurse and told her about the agreement with Dr. Knudsen, while handing my insurance card over to the nurse. We took the first date she offered, since I wasn't going anywhere in this wheelchair. When we got the appointment date, we headed left toward the elevators.

In the reception area, a cool stream of fresh air blew in with the revolving door. Five taxis lined up, waiting for customers when we came out.

Apart from the instructions to the driver, we made the trip home in silence, avoiding each other's glances.

The day was gray. A thin and steady rain escorted us to Farum.

Dad paid the fare and with the driver's assistance, took the wheelchair and helped me out of the car. The house had also aged; the beauty of the now-neglected garden was gone. The half-closed curtains, the cluttered mailbox filled with unread newspapers, and the unceasing rain presented a gloomy picture.

Dad and Mom looked at each other as if they suddenly remembered something.

"Taraji. We forgot ..." said Dad.

And suddenly I realized. It was Carson; he wasn't there anymore. Mom explained that he didn't suffer; he passed away on his pad.

I didn't say welcome to Carson, since he was already here when Mom and Dad brought me from Soweto, and I wasn't there either to say goodbye or thanks for everything. I didn't cry but the void was huge. I stood from the chair, took the crutches, and jumped my way forward.

Mom tried to hold me but I heard Dad tell her that I needed to be alone. He was so right.

I wanted to reconnect with each corner of the house. As I moved forward, I opened every door on my way to my bedroom just to recapture smells and images.

Everything was pretty much the same, but not me.

When I opened the door of my bedroom, it was as if time had stood still. The bunch of clothes was still lying on the bed. I recalled that I had been indecisive about what to wear the night of the concert. The receipts

I fished from my bag were still scattered on the nightstand. The laptop on the desk, to the right, the unfinished Suzanne Collins novel on top of a bunch of other books waiting to be read. Chaos reigned on my bed. I pushed everything aside except the garments and dropped onto the bed, using the pile of clothes as a cushion. I cried for Carson, for the accident, for the pain I had caused my parents, and because I missed Nick.

I think I heard Mom close to the door but she didn't come in. After a while, she walked away and I fell asleep, exhausted by weeping.

February 2014

I WASN'T READY to give up on Nick, so after a long process of healing and forgiveness, he gave me another chance.

It wasn't official, but we were together as much as we could be.

"Nick, what if I fall?" I asked, pulling the running gloves on my hands.

"I'll help you up," he shrugged, lacing the running chip to his shoe. "I'll wait for everyone to run past me. It's just five miles."

"Just," I repeated with a hint of irony, pulling the running beanie into place.

The music blared through the speakers and most of the runners were warming up. It was the first race of the year. The snow piled up on both sides of the sidewalk.

I spotted Mom and Dad from where we were standing and a wave of gratitude moistened my eyes. They were there, waving flags to cheer us on. They rescued me from a life without opportunities on the other side of the world. They forgave all my transgressions and were here today, supporting me.

Today, I would be the last one to run from the start line and maybe the very last to cross the finish line, but to them it would be like I just ran a marathon in the Olympic Games.

The shot rang and the digital watch started, too. The mass of elite runners was off.

"Nick, I think I'll be able to keep your pace."

"Really? That's good news, as you have to be fit when we fly to Soweto to find your family," Nick warned me.

"Sure," I said, smiling back at him.
A blast of cold air whipped us as we dried our runny noses.
I waved to Mom and Dad and they waved back.
Nick and I jogged to catch up with the other runners, holding hands.

Glossary

Alijuuna – non-Wayuu person, a foreigner to Wayuu people

Ambal – the national flower of Sri Lanka, this water lily is usually violet or fuchsia.

Amma – Mom

Anülü – loom

Appa – Dad

Avarakkai kootu – a side dish made in South Asia, which can be eaten with rice, is usually made with gourd, cabbage, Indian broad beans ground spices and coconut.

Brinjals – eggplant/aubergine

Chandbalis – earrings

Chicha maya – a party to celebrate the end of a girl's seclusion at the onset of puberty

Chirrinchi – alcoholic beverage used in special celebrations

Choli – an upper garment worn with the Indian *sari*

Dharavi – a district situated between Mumbai's two main suburban railway lines and is considered the world's largest slum

Ebi gyoza – a Japanese side dish that consists of dumplings with shrimps and vegetables, served with soy sauce with chili and garlic

Ebi katsu – a Japanese side dish with deep-fried shrimps, served with chili and garlic sauce and garnished with lime

Epieyu – Wayuu clan represented by the vulture, also related to death

Hagrid – fictional character in the Harry Potter series characterized for being a half-human, half-giant

Iyengar Brahmin – Hindu upper caste of Tamil origin that follows the Visishtadvaita philosophy promulgated by Sri Ramanujacharya

Jaggery – brown sugar

Jepira – heaven or the place where the deceased rest in peace

Jeyutse – white verbena flower

Juya – rain

239

Luthier – a person who makes or repairs string instruments: guitar, violin, etc.

Majayut – the transition process of the Wayuu girl after puberty, where she becomes ready to get married and start a family

Kothu Roti – Sri Lankan dish consisting of chopped vegetables mixed with curry sauce

Mareygua – God

Melakaar – drummers

Mulligatawny – vegetable soup

Piache – healer

Pooja – Hindu ritual that comprises offerings to various deities

Poorali – warrior

Sari – a South Asian garment for women, which consists of a drape of several yards in lenght

Sarong – fabric wrapped around the waist and worn by men and women in South Asia

Senkeyuu – twins

Shalwar Kameez – traditional dress from South and Central Asia consisting of pajama-like trousers and a tunic

Shiatapünaa – the half of a thing

Silmarillion – a narrative collection of five parts within the fantasy genre by J.R.R. Tolkien.

Samosas – A dish where savory vegetables, and sometimes meat are wrapped in a baked pastry. Very common in Pakistan and India

Tamarai – lotus flower and purity symbol

Tamby – little brother

Thaali – nuptial necklace

Tostones – fried slices of unripe plantain

Tsunami – Seismic sea wave

UEFA – Union of European Football Association

UNHCR – stands for United Nations High Commissioner for Refugees the UN refugee agency

Upma kozha kattai – steamed rice balls

Uriana – Wayuu clan represented by the jaguar

Vazhaipoo usii – curry side dish made with lentils and vegetables

Vibhuti – sacred ashes

Walekerü – spider , the art of weaving

Warepo – tiny shells used as bait by fishermen

Wayuu –an American Indian ethnic group, inhabiting the La Guajira Peninsula straddling the Venezuela-Colombia border

Wayuunaki – the language of the Wayuu people

Yaki udon – Japanese dish consisting of fried noodles, vegetables, chicken and curry sauce

Yaki soba yasai – Japanese dish consisting of fried wheat noodles, vegetables, sesame seeds and coriander vinegar

Yeye – the name of Yonna's rag doll

Yonna – dance

Yiiitüwaa – lonely

Zapuana – Wayuu clan represented by the curfew. It also announces the rain.

About the Author

Belangela, in one way or another, has always been around books. So it is no surprise to her that she eventually became a writer as a way of extending her love of reading. However, the path to get there wasn't always clear.

Born into a family of readers, Belangela discovered her passion for literature at a very young age. She could never get enough of the stories, from Gabriel García Marquez to Agatha Christie and Charles Dickens, among many others. She has never known a time when she wasn't reading or dreaming about writing stories.

Born in Caracas, Venezuela, she is the fourth of five children. Belangela became a Danish citizen many years ago and now resides in Denmark with her husband, embarking on the blessed quest of raising their autistic son. She finds her creative juices by running and enjoying nature.

Belangela was awarded a grant from Rieck-Andersens Familiefond to translate *The Child of Dawn* into Danish. She is the multigenre author of *The Child of Dawn* (nonfiction) and the *Truths of Illusion* series (fiction).

She is also a member of the Alliance of Independent Authors and an affiliate of the Association of Independent Authors.